LIFE'S SIMPLE PLEASURES

She was facing him now, her cool look gone and smiling a little. "Of course it's loaded."

"You going to shoot something?"

"We could. Windows are good."

"So you brought a gun to shoot at windows."

"And boats. Boats are fun."

"I imagine they would be. How about cars?"

"I didn't think about cars." She seemed pleasantly surprised. "Isn't that funny?"

"Yeah, that is funny."

"I just wanted you to know we have it."

"There's a difference," Ryan said, "between breaking and entering and armed robbery."

"And there's a difference between seventy-eight dollars and fifty thousand dollars," Nancy said. "How badly do you want it?"

THE BIG BOUNCE

Also by Elmore Leonard

Hombre
The Moonshine War
Valdez is Coming
Forty Lashes Less One
Fifty-Two Pickup
3:10 to Yuma
Swag
The Hunted *(published by Mysterious Press)*
Mr. Majestyk *(published by Mysterious Press)*
Unknown Man No. 89
The Switch
Gunsights
Gold Coast
City Primeval: High Noon in Detroit
Split Images
Cat Chaser
Stick
La Brava
Glitz *(published by Warner Books)*

THE BIG
BOUNCE

ELMORE
LEONARD

THE MYSTERIOUS PRESS • **New York**

MYSTERIOUS PRESS EDITION

Copyright © 1969 by Elmore Leonard
All rights reserved.

This Mysterious Press Edition is published by arrangement with the author.

Mysterious Press books are published in association with Warner Books, Inc.
666 Fifth Avenue
New York, N.Y. 10103
W A Warner Communications Company

Printed in the United States of America

First Mysterious Press Printing: September, 1986

10 9 8 7 6 5 4 3 2 1

ONE

THEY WERE WATCHING RYAN BEAT UP THE
Mexican crew leader on 16mm Commercial Ektachrome.
Three of them in the basement room of the Holden
County courthouse: the assistant county prosecutor, who
had brought the film; a uniformed officer from the
sheriff's department operating the projector; and Mr.
Walter Majestyk, the justice of the peace from Geneva
Beach.

Right now they were watching Ryan holding the soft-
ball bat, bringing it up to his shoulder and not taking his
eyes from Luis Camacho, who was beyond him on the
screen, crouched and edging to the side but gradually, it
seemed, closing in on Ryan.

"The guy's doing a movie on migrant workers," the assistant prosecutor said. "He happens to be there, he gets
the whole thing."

"There was a picture in the paper," Mr. Majestyk said.

"The same guy. He ran out of movie film and started
shooting with his Rollei."

On the screen Ryan was moving with Camacho, following him closely; he seemed about to swing, starting to
come through with it. Camacho lunged and pulled back;
Ryan checked his swing and chopped, and the assistant
prosecutor said, "Hold it there."

The sheriff's patrolman flicked a switch on the projector and the action on the screen stopped, slightly out of
focus.

"Do you see a knife?"

"He's behind him," Mr. Majestyk said. "You can't
tell."

The action continued, coming into focus: Camacho

5

still edging, holding his left arm tight to his side, and Ryan moving with him. Ryan was raising the bat again, his hands coming back to his shoulder, and the assistant prosecutor said, "Right there. The one that broke his jaw."

The stopped-action on the screen showed Ryan coming through with the bat, stepping with the swing, body twisting and arm muscles tight and straight and wrists turning as he laid the bat against the side of Luis Camacho's face. The face did not resemble a human face but a wood-carved face, an Aztec doll face without eyes or before the eyes were painted in. Camacho's wraparound hellcat sunglasses were hanging in space but still hooked to one ear, and though the framing of the picture did not show his lower legs, Camacho seemed to be off the ground hunch-shouldered, suspended in air.

"Larry," the assistant prosecutor said to the sheriff's patrolman, "keep that but give me some light. Walter, I want to read you Luis Camacho's statement."

The overhead fluorescent light washed the sharpness and detail from the figures on the screen, but the action remained clear. Mr. Majestyk, the justice of the peace from Geneva Beach, blinked twice as the light came to full brightness but kept his eyes on Jack Ryan.

"He gives his name," the assistant prosecutor began, "and when it happened, July twenty-sixth, about seven P.M., and then Officer J. R. Coleman says: 'Tell us in your own words what happened.' Walter, you listening?"

"Sure, go on."

"Camacho: 'After supper I went out to the bus and waited, as Ryan had promised to do some repair work on it for me. When he did not appear, I looked for him and found him in the field where some of the men and kids were playing baseball. The men had some beer and most of them were playing baseball. Ryan was with them, though he wasn't playing. There were some girls there Ryan was talking to. I asked him why he was not fixing the bus and he said something back that is unprintable. I reminded him that servicing the bus was part of his job, but he told me again to do the unprintable thing. One reason——"

6

"Excuse me," Mr. Majestyk said. "Larry, are those the words the guy used?"

The sheriff's officer hesitated. "They're, you know, writing words, the way you write it in a report."

"What'd Ryan tell him?"

"To go bag his ass."

"What's unprintable about that?"

"Walter—" The assistant prosecutor was looking at Mr. Majestyk, marking his place with the tip of his ball-point pen. "Camacho goes on to say: 'One reason I allowed him to join my crew in San Antonio was because he said he was a mechanic and could fix the bus if it broke down. I hired him but was suspicious because I believed all he wanted was a free trip as far as Detroit——'"

"He's from Detroit?" Mr. Majestyk seemed surprised.

"From Highland Park," the assistant prosecutor said. "The same thing. So then Camacho says: 'When I asked him again to fix the bus, he picked up the bat and told me to get out of there or he would knock my head off. I told him to put down the bat and we would settle this, but he came at me with it. Before I could defend myself or disarm him, he struck me in the arm and in the face.'" The assistant prosecutor paused. "That's the part, Walter. Listen. 'Before I could defend myself or disarm him ——.'"

"He got flattened," Mr. Majestyk said.

"'——he struck me in the arm and in the face. I fell to the ground but was not unconscious. I remember many of the people there looking down at me. When the police came, they called an ambulance and I was taken to the hospital at Holden, Michigan.'" The assistant prosecutor went on, reading it faster, "'This statement is sworn to before witnesses and bears my signature that all facts related are true and took place as I have described them.'" The assistant prosecutor straightened, looking at the Geneva Beach justice of the peace. "Walter, what do you think?"

Mr. Majestyk nodded, looking at the washed-out image on the screen. "I think he's got a level swing, but maybe he pulls too much."

7

Bob Rogers Jr. didn't bring Ryan's pay envelope until almost half past eleven Sunday morning. He told J. R. Coleman, the sheriff's officer on duty, what it was and who it was for and Coleman said he thought it was supposed to have been dropped off yesterday; they were waiting to get rid of this guy Ryan. Bob Jr. said he was busy yesterday and that another day in jail wasn't going to hurt Ryan any. He left the envelope on the counter and went out adjusting his curled-brim straw cowboy hat, loosening it on his head and setting it straight as he walked down the courthouse steps and across the street to the dark green pickup truck. He'd have about fifteen minutes to wait, so he U-turned and drove up Holden's main street to Rexall's and bought a pack of cigarettes and the big Sunday edition of the *Detroit Free Press*. By the time Bob Jr. got back to the courthouse, U-turning north again and pulling up in the no parking zone, he figured they'd be just about now giving Ryan his shoelaces and telling him to take off.

"Sign it at the bottom," J. R. Coleman said. He waited until Ryan had signed the form before he took Ryan's wallet, belt, and pay envelope out of a wire basket and laid them on the counter.

When Ryan opened the wallet and began counting the three one-dollar bills inside, J. R. Coleman gave him a no-expression look and kept staring while Ryan worked his belt through the loops of his khaki pants and buckled it and shoved the wallet into his back pocket. Ryan picked up the pay envelope then and looked at it.

"That's from the company. They dropped it off," J. R. Coleman told him.

"It isn't sealed."

"It wasn't sealed when they brought it."

Ryan read the pay period and the amount typed on the envelope. He pulled out the bills and counted fifty-seven dollars.

"That'll get you home," J. R. Coleman said. "Two blocks up's the Greyhound station."

Ryan folded the envelope and put it in his shirt pocket. He hesitated then and began feeling his pants pockets, his gaze moving over the counter surface. As he looked up at J. R. Coleman he said, "I had a comb."

"There isn't any comb here."

"I know there isn't. Why would anybody want to swipe a comb?"

"You didn't have a comb."

"No, I had one. I always have a comb."

"If it isn't here, you never had one."

"You can buy a new comb for ten cents," Ryan said. "A clean one. Why would anybody steal somebody else's comb?"

J. R. Coleman said, "I'll put you on the bus myself if you want me to."

"That's all right," Ryan said. "I'll see you."

"You better not," J. R. Coleman said.

Bob Rogers Jr. waited for Ryan to spot the pickup truck. He couldn't miss it with the white-lettered sign on the door: RITCHIE FOODS, INC., GENEVA BEACH, MICH. But Ryan was looking around, up at the trees and up the street, acting casual as he came down the courthouse steps. Bob Jr. sat with his elbow out the window. As Ryan approached the truck Bob Jr. adjusted his straw cowboy hat, raising the funneled brim and squaring it over his eyes, then laid his wrist over the top of the steering wheel, resting it there. He knew Ryan was going to open the door and he let him do it, let him get that far.

"You wanted a ride somewhere?"

Ryan looked up at him. "You're going north, aren't you?"

"That's right," Bob Jr. said. "But you're going south. One hundred and fifty miles due south to Detroit."

"I thought I'd get my gear first."

"You don't need your gear. All you need's a bus ticket. Or go over cross the street and stick your thumb out."

Ryan looked up the street north, frowning in the sunlight, at the stores lining the street and the cars angle-parked in front. He looked at Bob Jr. again and said, "You got a cigarette?"

"No, I don't."

"What's the square thing in your pocket?"

9

"That's a square thing in my pocket," Bob Jr. said.

"Well, I'll see you." Ryan slammed the door and started along the sidewalk.

Bob Jr. watched him. He waited until Ryan was almost to the corner before flicking the column shift with the tip of his finger and edging along close to the curb, his hands resting lightly on the thin steering wheel. When he was even with Ryan, he said, "Hey, boy, I wasn't finished talking to you." He rolled past him before stopping so Ryan would have to come up to him.

"I want to tell you something."

"Go ahead."

"Come here a little closer, I don't have to shout." Bob Jr. folded the Sunday paper next to him and leaned toward the window with his arm on the backrest of the seat.

"What?" Ryan said.

"Listen, the two weeks you lived with the spiks we never did talk much, did we?"

"I don't guess we did."

"That's right. So you don't know me, do you?"

Ryan shook his head, waiting.

"We never talked because I couldn't think of any reason I needed to talk to you," Bob Jr. said. "But I'll tell you something now. Go on home. I'll tell you it for your own good, because if you're not a white man, at least you look like a white man and I'll give you that much credit."

Ryan kept his mouth shut, staring at the grown man with the cowboy hat down over his eyes, the farm-hick Geneva Beach hot dog with the big arms and thirty pounds and maybe ten more years of experience on his side. And a pure white forehead, Ryan was thinking, if he ever took that dumb hat off. He had never seen Bob Jr. without the hat.

"You don't work for me no more," Bob Jr. was saying, "so legally you don't have to do what I tell you. But I'll give you the best reason I know for clearing out as quick as you can. You know what it is?"

Jesus Christ, Ryan thought. He said, "No. What?"

"Lou Camacho." Bob Jr. paused to let it sink in. "You don't beat up a crew leader in front of his men. He finds

10

out you're still here, he'll have somebody stick a knife in you so fast you won't even feel it go in."

"I hadn't thought of that," Ryan said.

"That happens and I'm up to my ass in so many sheriff's cops and state police, I don't get my cucumbers in till Christmas," Bob Jr. said. You see what I mean?"

Ryan nodded. "I hadn't thought of the cucumbers, either."

"It's the reason you're a free man today," Bob Jr. said.

Ryan nodded again. "I see."

And Bob Jr. kept staring at him. "No, you don't see. You're too dumb. But I'll tell you," Bob Jr. said. "Ritchie Foods got you loose because Ritchie Foods makes pickles. They make sweet pickles and dills and hamburger slices and those little gerkins. They put the pickles in jars and sell them. But, boy, what they don't put in jars and sell are cucumbers. Big grown cucumbers. That means they got to get the cucumbers picked before they're full-grown. That means they got to hurry this time of year to get the crop in. But they ain't going to get it in with the goddamn pickers sitting around in any goddamn courtroom. You see it now?"

"Well, the quicker I get my gear, the quicker I'm gone." Ryan smiled his down-home smile for Bob Jr. "So why don't you give me a lift to the camp? I mean if you're going that way."

Bob Jr. shook his head to show what an effort it was getting through to this guy. He said finally, "All right. You pick up your stuff and take off. Right?"

"Yes, *sir*." Ryan grinned. "Thanks a lot."

On the way he read the front page of the Sunday funnies—Dick Tracy and Peanuts; Bob Jr. wouldn't let him open the paper and mess it up; he said he was taking it to Mr. Ritchie. It didn't matter to Ryan. It was only about six miles up to the camp, off the highway to the left. He wondered if Bob Jr. was going to drop him off and go on into Geneva Beach—another two miles north, where the highway ended abruptly on Lake Huron—but Bob Jr. made his turn at the gravel road that went in to the camp, maintaining his speed and holding tighter to keep the

11

pickup from sliding in the ruts. That was all right too. Let him show off if he wanted. Ryan felt good. When something was over, it always felt good. After seven days in the Holden jail, even the cucumber fields, spreading into the distance on both sides of the road, looked good. He could relax, take his time; wash up, get his stuff together, and walk back to the highway. By four or five this afternoon he should be in Detroit. He started thinking about what he'd do when he got home. Take a hot shower and eat, maybe go out after and have a few beers. Maybe just go to bed in a real bed for a change.

Up ahead now he could see the company buildings. They reminded him of a picture he'd seen in *Life* of a deserted World War II Army post—the weathered barracks and washhouse and latrines in a hard-packed clearing; gray walls standing beyond their time; boarded windows or pushed-out screens and old newspapers and candy wrappers caught in the weeds that grew close to the buildings. It was funny he didn't see any kids in the road. There were always kids. Not many grown people outside unless they were coming in or going out to the fields, but there were always kids; hundreds of them, it seemed like, among the eighty-seven families living here this season. He remembered then it was Sunday. The kids would be at Mass or getting ready for it or hiding out in the woods somewhere.

That was it. He saw people now crossing from the shacks to the elm trees that lined the left side of the road. The priest who came on Sunday always set up his card-table altar in the elm shade. He'd park his Olds over there off the road and put his vestments on behind the car while a couple of the women dressed the card table with a white cloth and a crucifix and the priest's missal.

"Right here," Ryan said.

"Which one?"

"The shed."

Bob grinned as he braked, looking back through the rear window. "The bachelor quarters." He let Ryan out, saying, "Remember, now—"

Ryan walked back toward the shed. He heard the pickup starting off and a moment later heard the squeal of brakes as it stopped again, but Ryan didn't look around. He'd seen enough of the hot dog and heard enough of him and as far as he was concerned, Bob Jr. was gone forever. He opened the door of the shed and went into the mildew-smelling gloom of the place. It had once housed machinery or equipment; now there were newspapers spread over the dirt floor and the papers covered with pieces of burlap and an old straw rug. Three of them had lived in here. Now Billy Ruiz and Frank Pizarro could have it to themselves. He was glad they weren't here.

With the door open the first thing Ryan saw was the picture of himself on the wall clipped from the *Free Press* and pinned there between Al Kaline and Tony Oliva: Ryan holding the bat and Luis Camacho on the ground. The caption said:

MIGRANT WORKER HITS CREW LEADER FOR RAISE

A difference of opinion resulted in Jack C. Ryan putting the word to Luis Camacho, crew leader of a group of migrant cucumber pickers from Texas this month working in the fields of Michigan's Thumb area. Luis Camacho has been hospitalized. Ryan has been arraigned on a charge of felonious assault and is awaiting examination.

And something else about the guy making the movie who happened to be there, but Ryan didn't read the rest. He took off his shirt going over to his cot. His soap and safety razor were on a wall shelf; he picked them up in one hand, laid a towel over his shoulder, and went outside again.

The pickup was still in the road. Bob Jr. was out of it, beyond the front end and standing at the driver's side of a dark green Lincoln convertible pointing this way. Ryan had never seen the car with the top down before or—walking past the truck now—he had never seen it this close. Before it had always been a dark green car in the distance trailing dust. In the field they would straighten up over the cucumber plants; somebody would say, "There goes Mr. Ritchie," and they would stare after the car until it was gone.

Coming up past the truck, he got a good look at Mr.

13

Ritchie—not a bad-looking guy, about forty-five, sunglasses and a high, tan forehead, his dark hair starting to go. Then he was looking at the girl next to Mr. Ritchie with the big round Audrey Hepburn sunglasses; she was reading the Sunday funnies and as Ryan watched her she moved her dark hair away from her face with the tip of one finger: straight dark hair and long, down past her shoulders. She looked young enough to be Mr. Ritchie's daughter, but for some reason Ryan knew she wasn't.

Mr. Ritchie and Bob Jr. were watching him and now, one hand on the doorsill and the other on his hip, Bob Jr. gave a little side-motion jerk of his head to call Ryan over. He could hear music coming from the Lincoln convertible and off beyond them in the elm shade he could see the priest in green vestments and the people kneeling before the card-table altar.

Bob Jr. said, "Mr. Ritchie wants me to remind you you're not needed around here anymore."

"I'm going as soon as I clean up." He was aware of the girl looking up from the funnies on her lap, but he kept his eyes on Bob Jr. Then, when Mr. Ritchie spoke, he turned a little—with the towel over his shoulder and holding the end of it in front of him—to let the girl see his arm, the slim brown muscle bunched tight against the side of his chest.

"You're not a picker, are you?" Mr. Ritchie asked him.

"Not until a few weeks ago."

"Why'd you join them?"

"I needed something to do."

"Weren't you working in Texas?"

"I was playing ball for a while."

"Baseball?"

"Yes, sir, that's what you play in the summer."

Mr. Ritchie stared at him. "I understand you've been arrested before," he said then. "For what?"

"Well, one time resisting arrest." Ryan paused.

Mr. Ritchie said, "What else?"

"Another time B and E."

"What's B and E?" the girl said.

He looked right at her now, at the nice nose and the

14

big round sunglasses and the dark hair hanging close to her face.

"Breaking and Entering," Bob Jr. said.

The girl kept her eyes on Ryan. She said, "Oh," and again brushed aside her hair with the tip of one finger, a gentle, almost caressing gesture.

She would be nineteen or twenty, Ryan decided: slim and brown in white shorts and a striped blue and tan and white top that was like the top of a old-fashioned bathing suit, sitting there with her ankles tucked under her and moving the funnies now so Ryan or Bob Jr. or anybody who wanted to could see her nice tan legs.

"We're taking the boat out," Mr. Ritchie was saying to Bob Jr. "We might leave it at the beach place, I don't know."

Bob Jr. straightened. "Right. I'll have it picked up if you do."

"I'll be going back to Detroit about four thirty. You can check on the boat anytime after that."

"Right," Bob Jr. said. "You'll be back Friday?"

Mr. Ritchie was looking at Ryan. "We don't mean to keep you, if you want to pack and get going."

"I didn't know if you were through with me," Ryan said.

"We're through."

"Just remember," Bob Jr. said.

Ryan kept his eyes on Mr. Ritchie. "I was just wondering, you said you were driving to Detroit——"

"What'd I tell you!" The curled brim of Bob Jr.'s cowboy hat jutted toward him. "I said *now*. You know what that means? It means you leave *now*. This minute."

Ryan felt the girl watching him. His gaze shifted from Mr. Ritchie's solemn expression and he gave her the Jack Ryan nice-guy grin and shrugged and, just as he saw her begin to smile, walked off toward the washhouse.

When he came out into the sunlight again, shaved, cleaner, feeling pretty good, the convertible and the pickup were gone. He glanced over toward the elm shade at the priest in green vestments and the people kneeling before the card-table altar and he felt a little funny going by with his shirt off. He wanted to hurry, but

15

he made himself take his time. Hell, he wasn't in church. If the priest wanted to use this place as a church, that was up to him. Faintly, far away, he heard the words *"Sursum corda"* and the deeper sound of the people responding *"Habemus ad Dominum."* The priest did not speak Spanish and the people had persuaded him, weeks before, to say the Mass in Latin. *"Gratias agamus Domino, deo nostro,"* the priest said.

Dignum et justum est. Ryan heard the words in his mind. He had about fifteen minutes to get out while they were still at Mass. Some of the people who had become his friends would stand out in the sun talking to him forever if he let them. He didn't see Marlene Desea but decided she must be over in the elms. It would be just as well he didn't see her. He hadn't promised Marlene anything, but he didn't know what he'd say to her and he'd probably end up telling her he'd be down to San Antonio to see her and a lot of crap like that. He didn't worry about Billy Ruiz or Frank Pizarro. He didn't give them a thought until he saw Pizarro's panel truck, a blue '56 Ford turning purple and rusting out along the under edge of the body and wheel housings.

They were waiting for him inside the shed, Billy grinning at him with his awful teeth and Frank Pizarro stretched out on a cot in his boots and sunglasses.

Billy Ruiz said, "Hey, Frank, look who's here."

Pizarro was looking directly at Ryan; still he raised his head a little, acting it out. "Man, just in time, uh?"

"Like he know what we found," Billy Ruiz said.

"Sure," Pizarro said. "He got a nose for it."

Ryan spread open his canvas suit-pack on his cot. He put on a clean shirt and stuffed everything else he owned into the bag.

"He think he's leaving," Pizarro said. "We better tell him what we found."

16

TWO

"THERE IT IS," BILLY RUIZ SAID. "IT'S BROWN,
you can't see it much in the trees."

"I see it," Ryan said.

"The people with the sailboat? They're from the house. And the ones making the fire, I think."

"How many would you say?"

"I don't know. Twenty cars. Frank say they must have start coming before noon."

"I like it so far," Ryan said. He was smoking a cigar, a thin one that was now half smoked. He looked all right with it because he was at ease; his jaw clamped it lightly and he didn't fool with it or keep blowing out smoke.

They were walking along the shoreline where the water would wash in and leave a strip of sand wet and smooth. They walked barefoot with their pants rolled to their knees and sneakers in their back pockets; they wore sunglasses and peaked fishing caps and walked along taking their time, taking it easy, two guys from one of the cottages or the public beach out getting a little exercise, looking around at the boats and the people on the beach, looking at the cottages that were up on the slope, back a good two hundred feet from the water. By now most of the swimmers and sunbathers had gone in, though there were children still playing and digging in the sand and a few people walking along the shore.

"How would you like some of that?" Billy Ruiz said. "The red two-piece."

"Maybe in a couple of years," Ryan said.

"Man, young and tender."

"There's one."

The girl was coming down from a beach-front store.

17

She wore sunglasses and a white sweatshirt that reached to her tan thighs and covered her bathing suit.

"You can't see what she's got," Billy Ruiz said.

"She moves nice."

"Now you can see the house good." Billy Ruiz said.

The house was a brown-shingled, two-story house that seemed as old and permanent as the pines closing in on it. A square of white interrupted the dim look of the house, a sign, a canvas banner strung between two of the porch posts. It became a sign as they drew nearer the house.

ANNUAL ALPHA CHI ALUMNI OUTING—red letters on the white field. There were a few people on the porch, but most of the alumni and their wives seemed to be on the beach; in a gypsy camp of lounge chairs and beach towels or in small groups standing by the beached sailboat and around the cookfire they were building, each one holding, elbow at his side, a paper cup or a bottle of beer.

"I like it," Ryan said. He squinted toward the house, chewing a little on the end of the cigar.

"We better cut up, uh, before we get there?"

"No, we'll walk past. Then up through the trees."

"I wouldn't mind another beer."

"Just take it easy."

They approached the group by the sailboat. Billy Ruiz started to walk out into the water to go around them, but Ryan touched his arm and he followed Ryan past them on the beach side, Ryan pausing to look at the fiberglass catamaran hulls of the boat and Billy Ruiz thinking, God, he's going to talk to them. When they were beyond the people, Ruiz said, "You *want* them to see you?"

"I never saw a boat like that," Ryan said. "You see it? Like two hulls."

"Man, why don't you ask them for a ride?"

Ryan grinned with the cigar in his mouth, glancing back at the house. "Come on, this is far enough." And now they crossed the beach, climbing the rise to a deserted stretch of frontage that was overgrown with brush and young pines. They stopped to put on their shoes, then made their way through the trees to the private drive behind the cottages. They could hear cars passing on the highway, the Shore Road off beyond a stand of trees, but they couldn't see the cars from here. The private drive was good and private: no cars except for the ones parked near the brown house, parked in the yard and on both sides of the road and in front of the sign nailed to a tree. YOU'RE HERE! the sign said, and something smaller beneath the two words.

"A nice turnout," Ryan said. "A nice active group."

Billy Ruiz was looking up the drive toward the cars. "That goddamn Pizarro," he said.

Ryan felt a little tight feeling in his stomach, but it was natural and there wasn't anything you could do about it; he stood at ease with his hands in his pockets and watched Billy Ruiz: Ruiz squinting and frowning, his bony shoulders hunched, walking a few steps and turning, kicking a stone, pulling a cigarette out of his shirt pocket now, and taking three matches to light it.

It was about a quarter after four. If he had left the camp by one, he would be in Detroit now. But Pizarro and Billy Ruiz had talked him out of it. They had stopped in a place about noon for cigarettes and all these guys were in the store buying cases of beer and ice and all kinds of mixes. Pizarro and Billy Ruiz had followed them to the house on the beach and there it was, man, waiting for them, just like they had talked about it over the wine and tequila all those Saturday nights. Man, he couldn't go home now. Later, maybe. Now he had to at least look at it. So they had picked up a case of cold beer and had driven past the place, out to the state park, where they drank three beers each and talked about it, Ryan wanting Pizarro to go in the house with him but Pizarro insisting that he drive the truck because it was his truck. ("You can drive after," Ryan had said. But Pizarro had said no, "I drive it all the time. Nobody else." "Frank," Ryan had said, "if Billy dents the son of a bitch, we'll pay you for it." No, Pizarro wasn't having any of that. "I drive," he had said, "Nobody else.") All right, Ryan had thought. No arguing. It would have been good to let him have one in the mouth and wake him up, but the better thing was to get it over with and get out. So he and Billy Ruiz had taken off down the beach.

"He'll be here," Ryan said now.

"He don't know we're going to take so long."

"Then, what're you blaming him for?" As he said it they heard a car door slam and saw the car backing out of the yard behind the brown house. It moved off in the other direction.

Billy Ruiz stood rigid. "Where is he going?"

"He's going to get some mustard," Ryan said. "They brought the charcoal and the hamburger and the paper plates, but his wife forgot the mustard."

He was watching the car and saw it edge close to the side of the road as Pizarro's panel truck, coming this way, squeezed past. "Here comes a friend of ours," Ryan said. He heard Billy Ruiz let his breath out in a sigh of cigarette smoke and both of them stood waiting for the truck.

"You were supposed to be here," Pizarro said. "I come by before, you're not here."

"It took longer than we thought." Ryan said. "All right?" The first and last time, he was thinking, and said to Pizarro, "You wait here. If somebody comes, you still wait here."

"What if it's cops?"

"What if we forget the whole thing?"

"Listen, I want to be sure. That's all."

"Who's sure?" Ryan said. He went to the back of the truck and brought out the beer case. The full bottles and empties had been taken out. He glanced at Billy Ruiz and the two of them walked away from the truck toward the brown house, Ryan still with the little stub of cigar in his mouth.

"What if somebody's watching?" Billy Ruiz asked.

Never again, Ryan thought. He said, "Billy, what are we doing? We're delivering beer."

They walked past the cars parked in the road, cut between them, and were in the yard. "Here's where you wait," Ryan said. "You watch for the sign. If I don't give you the sign, you don't come. But if I give it to you, then you come *now*, you understand?"

20

Billy Ruiz nodded, concentrating. He watched Ryan go up a narrow aisle between the cars parked in the yard, carrying the beer case now with both hands as if it were full. He watched Ryan step up on the porch, put the case down, and knock on the screen door. Ryan waited. He put his face close to the screen, shading out the light with one hand. He picked up the case again and went inside.

Billy Ruiz waited. This, he knew would be the worst part. He heard cars on the Shore Road beyond the trees. He turned and looked up and down the private drive and saw Frank Pizarro standing by the truck, looking this way. Get inside! God, the idiot, standing there! Ruiz's gaze swung to the house and now there was no time to worry about Frank Pizarro. Ryan was standing in the doorway motioning to him. He hurried past the cars and up onto the porch, trusting Ryan now, putting it all in his hands.

Ryan picked the cigar stub from his mouth and drew Billy Ruiz close to him with a hand on his shoulder.

"Somebody's in the living room," Ryan said. "But I think we're all right. It's at the end of the hall and the stairs are about halfway. I go up first. You bring the case and follow me but not right behind. If you hear me talking to anybody, walk out. I mean walk."

That was it. Simple. Like a huddle in a touch football game. You go out deep and cut. You go short and button-hook. I'll throw to whoever's clear. Maybe it'll work, maybe it won't.

Billy Ruiz followed Ryan through the kitchen he had never seen before to the hall and now heard a voice in the living room, a woman's voice, and laughter. The hall was dim, but the stairs were in light that came through two windows at the landing. He saw Ryan go up and turn the corner. He followed and when he reached the upstairs hall, Ryan had already found the room where the men of the Alpha Chi alumni had changed into their bathing trunks. Ryan stepped in and locked it.

"Look in the bathroom," Ryan said. He took the beer case from Ruiz and placed it on the bed, laid his cigar stub in an ashtray on the nightstand, and began going through the shorts and trousers on the bed and chairs and

21

on the dresser, removing the wallets and dropping them in the beer case, then checking the pockets for loose bills; he did not take silver. He looked around the room as he fished through the pockets, noticing the two windows that would be at the side and the back of the house. Good. The back window would open onto the porch roof.

"Another bedroom," Billy Ruiz said. He seemed surprised, but part of it was fright. "The women's clothes are in there."

"I'll check it," Ryan said. "You wait here." He moved through the bath to the adjoining bedroom, closed the door to the hall and locked it and turned to the clothes on the bed, in neat piles and messy piles, just as the men's were. Who goes with who? Ryan thought. That would be something if you had time. Try to match them up. There were seven purses on the dresser; he carried them into the men's bedroom and dropped them on the bed and began removing the wallets from those that had wallets and checking side pockets for rolled-up wads of bills. They would take all the wallets and go through them later.

When he had cleaned out the purses, he took them back to the women's bedroom. Just once have all the purses in one place. Man. Seven here, the rest would be scattered all over the house and when it's time to go, a couple of the women, half loaded, will be running around saying, "I can't find my purse." And the guy, more in the bag than his wife, will say, "Well, where did you put it?" He checked sweater pockets quickly but found nothing except tissues and a couple of combs.

He paused in the bathroom to open the medicine cabinet. It was funny about medicine cabinets—all the stuff in them, medicines and cosmetics he had never seen before. He took a bottle of Jade East from the shelf and studied the label going into the bedroom.

Billy Ruiz looked at him, still with wide-open eyes. "What are you doing?" Ryan was rubbing the after-shave lotion over his jaw.

One of Ryan's fingers, upright, moved to his mouth and he stood still. He waited, and then began rescrewing the cap gently and dropped the bottle to the bed. There

22

was a sound from the stairs. Steps now in the hall. The doorknob turned.

Ryan, on the far side of the bed from the door, saw the doorknob and Ruiz's expression at the same time. Get to him, Ryan thought. Get a hand on him. He moved quietly to Ruiz's side at the foot of the bed and touched his arm, held it.

The knob turned again, back and forth; the knob was jiggled, pushed, and pulled.

"Hey, who's in there?" A pause. "Come on, let me in."

Ryan waited. He said, "Just a minute," and moved to the closet and began going through the sweaters and sport coats and pants hanging inside. He found three billfolds and put them in the beer case.

"What're you doing? I got to go to the bathroom."

"Use the other one."

"Hey, who is it?"

"Look, we'll . . . get out if you'll go away."

"Who's *we?*"

Silence. Let it sink in, Ryan thought. He wants to say something, but now he's not sure.

Ryan waited until he heard steps in the hall and a door close—the other bathroom. Now, Ryan thought, he'll open it again quietly, the son of a bitch, and wait to see who comes out. How about a guy like that?

"Time to go," Ryan said. He moved to the back window that looked out on the porch, unfastened the screen, and motioned Ruiz to get the beer case. They climbed out. Ryan went down on his stomach at the edge of the roof and listened, not moving. After this he did not hesitate again; he rolled over the edge holding the gutter and dropped. Billy Ruiz lowered the beer case to him and followed and they went into the brush and trees at the side of the house, pointing now toward the private drive and Pizarro's truck. They walked, they didn't hurry; they walked because Ryan said that's the way it was done.

23

THREE

FRANK PIZARRO TURNED LEFT ON THE
Shore Road toward Geneva Beach four miles away and
was doing forty as he shifted into third gear. Ryan, behind him in the panel compartment, sitting on his canvas
suit-pack and opening the beer case, touched Pizarro's
shoulder.

"Hey, come on."

Pizarro glanced at the outside rearview mirror, then at
the two-lane road ahead and now he had to slow down
because of the Sunday-afternoon traffic. Ryan watched
through the windshield. No hurry. Never hurry. He
straightened to look out the back window. Nothing. A
few cars trailing, creeping along. Billy Ruiz moved in
closer on his knees as Ryan emptied the beer case, dumping the wallets and billfolds on the floor, and Billy Ruiz
spread them out with his hands, playing with them, enjoy-
ing the feel of them.

"How many do you think?" Ruiz said.

"I don't know. Thirty-five."

"We missed some."

"Some. Some guys didn't change. Or they changed in
another room."

Billy Ruiz grinned. "I'd like to see that guy's face, the
one in the bathroom, uh?"

They cleaned out the wallets one by one, going into the
card pockets and the cellophane sections to be sure, but
taking only the bills and putting the empty wallets back in
the beer case. Billy Ruiz handed Ryan what he had
found. Ryan separated the bills by denominations,
stacked them again, and began counting.

"A good day," Ryan said.

Over his shoulder Pizarro said, "How much?"

"A good day," Ryan said again.

There was seven hundred and seventy dollars even. They had been lucky. Even with the uneasy feeling before, it had come off all right. Even the amount seemed like a sign of luck. Seven hundred and seventy.

He counted off two hundred dollars. "For Frank," Ryan said to Billy Ruiz. But he hesitated, held it. He counted off a hundred and handed him that much. He counted two hundred again. "This is for you."

"Hey"—Pizarro was holding the bills open on the steering wheel—"what kind of cut is this?"

"Your cut," Ryan said.

"How much you get?"

"Seven hundred."

"And I get a hunnert, that's all?"

"That's scale for waiting in the truck."

"Man, I told you. I owe Camacho four hunnert fifty dollars."

"That's right," Ryan said. "You told me."

Billy Ruiz was staring at him. Ryan felt it and looked at the bony, yellowish face with its stained-looking, wide-open eyes.

"I didn't sit in no car," Billy Ruiz said.

"Are you complaining, Billy?"

"I went in with you."

"Would you have gone in without me?"

Ruiz said nothing. He stared out through the windshield now, watching the road and the car ahead of them. Ryan's eyes dropped to the money, folding it, but he could still see Billy Ruiz. The dumb bastard; the dumb cucumber picker. Ruiz wouldn't have gone near the house alone. He wouldn't have walked *past* it. Dumb skinny blank-eyed little weasel that tells you all the places he's been and how much he can drink and all the broads he's had, with his pants too long and sagging in the seat, too dumb to know how dumb he looks, how skinny ugly baggy-assed dumb.

He peeled two twenties and a ten from the roll of bills

and nudged Ruiz's arm. Ruiz looked at him with the blank look. He looked down at the money and he grinned. He was happy. Fifty bucks. God.

Pizarro could shove it. He was through with them now and everybody was paid.

But it stayed in his mind. You never should have let them into this, he thought, then told himself to forget it. In time this would be past him and he wouldn't worry about it or think about it again. Look at all the things you've done that you never think about anymore, he said to himself.

"Hey, this is the place," Billy Ruiz said. He was kneeling up against the front seat, his head lowered and pointing to the left side of the road. "See, the golf course along here. Then"—he waited as they moved past the fairways and scattered greens—"up there, see? The road goes in. See the sign?" It was an Old English-looking board sign hanging from a chain between two posts and painted green. On it in white letters were the words THE POINTE, and below them, smaller, PRIVATE.

"Remember, I was telling you?" Billy Ruiz said. "This is the place. All along here where the rich ones live. Man, they got homes back in there—big, big—Christ, make that brown one look like a goddamn chicken house."

Ryan looked out the back window as they passed the entrance road and continued along another stretch of fairways. He noticed the same cars following them.

"You've been back in there?"

"I tole you," Billy Ruiz answered. "Last year we go in take a look around, they kick us out."

"Who kicked you out?"

"I don't know. Some guy."

"Police?"

"No, no. Like a gatekeeper. There used to be a little house there where the road go in? He come after us."

"I don't know," Ryan said. "I'd have to see it."

"I tole you, it's perfect."

"If you say so." Let it die, Ryan thought. He hunched forward and watched the road ahead. In a couple of minutes it would be over; he'd pile out with his bag and that

26

would be it. But there was one more thing to make sure of.

He waited until they were passing the motels on the outskirts of Geneva Beach, passing the Putt-Putt Golf now and the Dairy Queen, and could see the stores and the signal light a couple of blocks ahead. The IGA supermarket was on the right.

"There," Ryan said. "You see the IGA?"

"It's closed," Pizarro said.

"Remember it." Ryan watched as they covered another block. Now he could see the PIER BAR sign on the left, the white building and the boat docks beyond it. Maybe a couple of beers, he thought. And something to eat. He'd still be in Detroit by nine.

"Right here," he said to Pizarro.

"What?"

"I'm leaving you," Ryan said.

"Man," Billy Ruiz said, "how can you go? We got things to do."

They were approaching the Shore Road-Main Street intersection and Pizarro was slowing down now for the traffic signal. "You go around the block to the back of the IGA store," Ryan told him. "You'll see a lot of boxes and junk piled up. That's where you dump the beer case. You got that? Nowhere else."

"Listen," Pizarro said, "I tole you, I got to make some more money." He was stopping now behind a car at the intersection.

Billy Ruiz was frowning. "What do you go for? We can make this every week."

"You and Frank do it," Ryan said. As the panel truck came to a full stop he had the rear door open and was out, dragging his canvas bag after him.

Billy Ruiz was close behind him, crouched in the open doorway now. "Wait a minute. Man, we should go somewhere and talk."

Ryan said, "Watch your fingers, Billy," and slammed the door. Walking across the street to the Pier Bar, he heard Pizarro call something and heard a car blowing its horn and then another one, but he didn't look back. No, sir, that was over.

Bob Jr. said, "What do you mean he took your keys?"

"I mean he took the keys," the girl said. "So I can't drive the Mustang."

"Well, sure, because of last week."

"The creep," the girl said.

"He doesn't want you getting in any more trouble."

"I like the way you stick up for him."

"Well," Bob Jr. said. "It's his car."

"It is not. It's in my name. I made sure of that, Charlie."

"Well, he gave it to you."

"Big deal."

"When do you go to court?"

"I don't know. Next month."

"I understand one of the boys is really hurt."

"That's too bad," the girl said.

"I guess it's his own fault."

"You bet it is," the girl said.

Bob Jr. eased lower in the white lounge chair. "Listen, why don't you come on over here?" he said to the girl, whose name was Nancy and who had been living in Mr. Ritchie's house since early June. "Why don't you sit down and relax a while?"

"I'm going to go in and get a sweater."

"Bring me one."

"None of Ray's would fit you."

"I was just kidding. I don't need any sweater."

He turned, shifting his weight, to watch Nancy walk toward the house. She could stand about ten pounds but, *damn*, that was a nice little compact can in the white shorts and the striped top you could see down, and she knew it too, whenever she bent over. He watched her slide open the glass door that led into the activities room. That's where the bar was. Maybe she'd bring out some drinks.

That'd be something. Get her to loosen up and relax. It was quiet now except for once in a while the faint, faraway sound of a boat motor; quiet and nice with the patio and swimming pool and most of the lawn in the shade; quiet and private with the stockade fence on both sides of the yard and, out in front, against the sky, the edge of the steep slope that dropped down to the beach: forty-eight steps and two landings. He ought to know because he had put the new stairway in the end of June with the two pickers helping him and Nancy lying around in the little two-piece outfit with her belly button showing. He had been coming back ever since.

Today he had waited until 5:30, giving Mr. Ritchie plenty of time to start back to Detroit. If Mr. Ritchie had still been here, Bob Jr. figured he could always say he'd come to check on the boat. Mr. Ritchie did that a lot on Sunday: he and Nancy would go out and fool around a couple of hours then tie up at the house instead of the yacht club so Mr. Ritchie could change, get right in his car, and head for Detroit. Then Bob Jr. would have to call the yacht club for somebody to come over and pick up the boat—a beauty sitting out there now, a thirty-eight footer, white with dark green trim, white and pickle green, like everything Mr. Ritchie owned: white house with a green sun deck over the lower level, green shrubs, green tile around the pool, green Mustang, green Lincoln, all the farm equipment green, a green and white Swiss-looking hunting lodge up back of the farm property. It was all right, Bob Jr. had decided, if you liked green and white, but his favorite colors, personally, were blue and gold, the colors of the uniforms they had worn at Holden Consolidated.

She came out in a light blue crew-neck sweater that looked nice with her dark hair, taking her time and not carrying a bottle or glasses, damn it. It was strange she walked so slow, a girl as itchy-bitchy as she generally was.

"I thought I had another set of keys," Nancy said, "but I don't."

"I'll tell you what. I'll let you use the pickup."

"That son of a bitch. He expects me to sit here all week waiting for him."

Bob Jr.'s head was turned to watch her. "Isn't that part of the deal?"

"The deal, Charlie, is none of your business."

"Why don't you get us some drinks?"

"I want to do something."

29

"Well, let's see," Bob Jr. said. "We could go out in the boat."

"I've been out in the boat."

"What do you do out there?"

Nancy stood with her arms folded, looking out past the edge of the bluff, at the lake that reached to the horizon. She didn't bother to answer him.

"You do some fishing?"

She gave him a look.

"I know what. You go swimming bare-ass and then he chases you around the boat."

"Right," Nancy said. "How did you know?"

"Come on, let's go out. Just till dark."

"Your wife will be wondering about you."

"She went down to Bad Axe to visit her mother."

"With all the little kiddies? While Daddy—what do you tell her daddy's doing?"

"Come on, let's go out in the boat."

"I don't *want* to go out in the boat."

"Then, get us something to drink. Hey, some Cold Ducks."

"I want to do something."

"That's something."

"I want to go out."

"And ride some boys off the road?"

She was looking at him now. "You wouldn't have enough nerve."

"I know something better to do."

"You wouldn't have the nerve to take me out," she said then. "Would you? You'll sneak in here when Ray's gone, but you wouldn't take me out, would you?"

"Like where?"

"*Out.* I don't know."

"There's no reason. You got everything you want right here."

"I want to go out," Nancy said. "Do you want to go out with me or do you want to go home?"

It was almost seven by the time they reached Geneva Beach. Bob Jr. said well, tell me what you want to do,

30

you want to do something so bad. Nancy told him she'd let him know.

"Well, if we're going driving, I got to get some cigarettes." Bob Jr. angled-parked near the drugstore and went inside.

Nancy waited in the pickup truck, her gaze moving slowly over the people who idled past on the sidewalk. After a minute or so she sat up on the seat and began combing her hair in the rearview mirror. When she stopped, the comb still in her hair, she edged to the side, looking past her own reflection. For a moment she sat still. Then she turned so she could look at them directly: Jack Ryan and the heavyset man standing by the restaurant across the street. They moved along the sidewalk, waited for the Shore Road light, and crossed over toward the Pier Bar.

When Bob Jr. came out of the drugstore, her hair was combed and she said to him, "I know where I want to go."

FOUR

WHEN NANCY HAYES WAS SIXTEEN SHE liked to babysit. She didn't have to babysit, she could have had a date almost any night of the week. She didn't need the money, either; her father sent her a check for $100 every month in an envelope marked PERSONAL that came the same day her mother received her alimony check. Nancy babysat because she liked to.

It was while she and her mother were living in Fort Lauderdale in a white $30,000 house with jalousy windows and terrazzo floors and a small curved swimming pool in the yard, not quite seven miles from the ocean.

Not far from them, on the other side of the Ocean Mile Shopping Center, the houses were larger, on canals, some with cruisers moored to the dock. The people who lived here were not year-round residents but stayed usually from January through Easter. They went to several parties a week and those with young children, if they were lucky, got Nancy Hayes to babysit for them. They liked Nancy: really a cute kid with the dark hair and brown eyes and cute little figure in her T-shirt and hiphuggers. She was also polite. She stayed awake. And she usually brought a book.

The book was a good touch. She would bring one of the Russians or an autobiography and leave it on the coffee table by the couch until it was time to go, moving her bookmark thirty or forty pages before the people came home. What Nancy liked to do the first few times she sat for someone was look through the house. She would wait until the children were asleep, then she would begin, usually in the living room, and work toward the master bedroom. Desks were good if they had letters in them or a checkbook to look through. Kitchens and dining rooms were boring. Florida or family rooms had possibilities only. But bedrooms were always fun.

Nancy never found anything really startling, like letters from a married man under the woman's underwear or dirty pictures in her husband's drawer. The closest she came to that was a copy of a nudist magazine beneath three layers of starched white shirts and—one other time —a revolver in with the socks and handkerchiefs. But the revolver wasn't loaded and there weren't any bullets in the drawer. It was usually that kind of letdown, expecting to find something and not finding it. Still, the actual looking was fun, the anticipation that she *might,* one of these evenings, discover something good.

Another thing Nancy liked to do was break things. She would drop a glass or a plate in the kitchen every once in a while, but the real bounce was breaking something expensive, a lamp or figurine or mirror. Though it couldn't be two houses in the same neighborhood or more than once in the same house—or at all if the child she was taking care of was old enough to talk. The best way was to sit

32

on the living room floor rolling a ball to the two-or three-year-old, then pick the ball up and throw it at a lamp. If she missed, she would keep trying. Eventually she would shatter the lamp and little Greg would be blamed. ("I'm terribly sorry Mrs. Peterson, he was pulling on the cord and before I could get to him——") Gosh, she was sorry.

Another thing that was fun she did with the fathers when they drove her home. She didn't always do it, or with all the fathers. To qualify, the father had to be in his thirties or early forties, a sharp dresser, good-looking in a middle-aged way and at least half in the bag each time he drove her home. To do it right required care and patience over a period of months, during a dozen or so rides home. The first time she would be very nice, her book in her lap, and not speak unless asked a direct question. If asked a question, it was usually about the book or how's school. Somehow, then, in answering—telling her grade in school or describing the book, which seemed pretty deep for a young girl—she would let him know she was going on seventeen. During the next several rides home she would be increasingly more at ease, friendly, outgoing, sincere; she would come off as a serious reader, a bright girl interested in what was going on in the world, especially the teen-age world with its changing fads and attitudes. Sometimes the discussion was so interesting they would arrive at Nancy's house and, parked in the drive, continue talking for another ten or fifteen minutes. Sooner or later then, usually between the fifth and eighth ride home, talking as they pulled into the drive, she would zap him.

It would be an apparently innocent question, part of their conversation. Like: "Do you think it's all right for teen-agers to make out?" He would act casual and ask her to define making out and she would say: "You know, parked somewhere."

"Well, if you're just parked, listening to the radio——"

"Of course I mean if they're in love, or if they feel at least a strong physical attraction."

"You wonder if it's all right for them to do a little smooching?"

"Uh-huh, not necessarily going all the way or sexing around too much, but maybe frenching and letting him touch you, you know, here."

Then the timing. Just as he said, "Well—" she would look at her watch and say, "Oh my gosh, I'd better get in!" And with a thanks-a-lot, slam the door in his face.

Then the next time steer the conversation or wait to see if he steered it to making out—or smooching or necking, as he called it. If he didn't she would move in quickly and zap him again.

"But why are boys always, you know, so anxious?"

"It's just the way they are physiologically. I suppose psychologically too."

Innocently, a sincere girl in search of knowledge: "Are older men that way?"

"Sure older men are. Not too old but older."

"I've wondered about that. Like young girls who marry older men."

"Well, if they're too old——"

"There was a movie star recently—I can't think of his name—he's fifty and the girl I think is twenty-two. That's, gosh, twenty-eight years difference!"

"If they get along, have mutual interests, a rapport, then why not?"

"Uh-huh. I guess so. If they love each other."

Now watch the serious, rationalizing father turning it over in his mind in the dark car with the dash lights and the radio low and her tan legs in the short shorts. "What are you, seventeen? That would be only eighteen years difference between us," he would say, knocking anywhere from three to six years from his age. "Could you imagine —say in a couple of years, and if I weren't married— could you imagine you and I going together?"

"I hadn't thought of it that way."

"But it could happen, couldn't it?"

"Gee, I guess it could."

Within one December to April season, six after-the-party, half-in-the-bag fathers, who lived within a mile of one another but were not acquainted (she made sure of that), had reached the verge and realized the clear possibility that cute little Nancy Hayes with the cute little

34

figure could be more to them than a babysitter. Three escaped: they did nothing about it; they seemed interested in her; they liked talking to her; they teased themselves with the possibility of her; but they did nothing about it.

Three did not escape.

One of them, taking Nancy home, turned off the road before reaching her street and rolled dead-engine into the willows that grew along a deserted stretch of canal. He pulled her to him across the console-glovebox between the bucket seats, with the faint sound of Sinatra coming from the instrument panel, and with a sad, aching look in his eyes kissed her gently, lingeringly on the mouth. When they parted, Nancy nestled close and put her head on his shoulder.

The second one happened to run into Nancy late one afternoon at the Ocean Mile Shopping Center, at the paperback rack in the drugstore, and asked her if she'd like a lift home; then, because it was such a terrific afternoon, asked if she'd like to drive over to Bahia Mar and watch the fishing boats come in. They stopped at Bahia Mar long enough to buy a sixpack and drove up the beach, almost to Pompano, where a row of new condominium apartments were under construction, empty concrete shells in the 5:30 sunlight, rising out of the cleared land. They parked in the close shadow of what would soon be the east wing of *The Castile* and the father drank three of the beers, giving her sips, bigger and bigger sips, telling her it was funny how much easier it was to talk to her than to his wife, how she seemed to understand him better. He was gentle when he put his arm around her and raised her chin gently but studied as he kissed her, his palm against her cheek. Her head tilted to his shoulder, her eyes warm and holding.

The third one came home from golf in the early afternoon to find his wife in Miami shopping and Nancy babysitting: Nancy in a dry two-piece white bathing suit watching the four-year-old at the shallow end of the pool. She could go now, but he asked her to stay awhile, to put the youngster in bed for his nap while he changed. The father had three gimlets and swam one length of the pool while Nancy watched from a lounge chair. He came out to stand over her dripping, sucking in his stomach as he rubbed a towel over his body. He said, hey, haven't you been in yet? Nancy said she had to go. The father said come on, don't be chicken. He pulled her up. Nancy fought him just enough, laughing, and felt him sneak a feel as he threw her in the pool. When she went into the house, he followed her, stopping in the kitchen to make another gimlet. Nancy went to the guest room, where she had changed. She closed the door, took off the top of her bathing suit and began drying her hair. She didn't have long to wait. He said, "Are you decent?" opening the door as he said it. Nancy squealed and turned away from him. In the dresser mirror she watched him come up behind her. She felt his hands on her hips, then slide around her waist. She let her head sink back to rest on his shoulder.

And to each of the three who did not escape, close to them, her head on their shoulders, she said, "Do you know what I'm going to do?"

Each one of the three whispered. "No. What are you going to do?"

And she answered, "I'm going to write to your wife and tell her you were seen taking advantage of a sixteen-year-old girl, that's what."

She did, too.

Ray Ritchie, father number two, the one who had taken Nancy for the ride up toward Pompano, looked at the note and said to his wife, "I like girls, you know that. But I draw the line." That would serve as his statement. Ray Ritchie almost always had something going on the side, from out-of-town weekends to downtown year-rounders, and he knew his wife wasn't going to make a case out of this one. He was busy, he traveled a lot, he had interests in several companies in addition to Ritchie Foods; his wife had a $150,000 home, live-in help, clubs, charge accounts, their one child in a good school and she could believe whatever she liked.

Nancy didn't see Ray Ritchie again until the next season. She wasn't babysitting anymore, she was working in a casual shop at Ocean Mile. This time when Ray Ritchie ran into her, he didn't take her to Bahia Mar or up toward Pompano. He took her to the Lucayan Beach Hotel on Grand Bahama for the weekend, Saturday through Tuesday.

The following 4th of July, Nancy was Miss˙Perky Pickle; she wore a dark green bathing suit and dark green high heels and rode through Geneva Beach behind the Holden Consolidated Marching Band, waving to everybody from the top of Ray Ritchie's Continental. In August she wrote to her mother to say she was taking a job in Ritchie Foods' P.R. department. She wrote the letter from her $400-a-month apartment overlooking the Detroit River.

As Miss Perky Pickle, she attended conventions, promotional parties, and store openings. She went to Cleveland, Chicago, and Minneapolis with Ray. She posed with Ritchie Foods' displays and passed out samples. She waited in hotel suites for Ray. She raced to airports with Ray. She sat with Ray and his group at bunny clubs and key clubs, usually the only girl at the table. She listened to the radio or record player all day when she was in the apartment. She switched her allegiance from the Hermits to the Loving Spoonful to the Blues Magoos and the Mamas and the Papas. She read *Vogue, Bazaar,* and *'Teen.* She walked around the apartment and looked at herself in the mirror. She looked out the window, at the winter stillness of the Detroit River, at the factory warehouse skyline of Windsor, Ontario. She fooled around with an account rep from Ritchie Foods' ad agency who pretended to be relaxed but kept looking toward the door. She sat alone weekends when Ray was in Fort Lauderdale with his family. She was thinking of going down herself, to see what old mom was doing, when Ray asked if she wanted to spend the summer at the beach house—he'd be up quite a bit and it would be cooler than Detroit.

There was sunlight in the windows and on the pale blue carpeting, an afternoon in late May, quiet in the apartment because Ray had turned off the radio when he came in. He had ten minutes to change and pack an overnight bag for Chicago; forty minutes to get to the airport.

37

She had fixed him a Scotch and soda and now sat on the couch while he changed his clothes, came out of the bedroom several times with the drink in his hand, took two phone calls and made a call, and finally stopped long enough to mention the beach house.

"What about your wife, doesn't she go up?"

"A couple of times, maybe. She stays home and plays golf. She plays golf every morning and drinks gin and tonic in the afternoon."

"What do I do when she comes?"

"You go to the hunting lodge. Or come back here if you want."

"Slip out the back door as she comes in the front."

"If you don't like the way it is," Ray Ritchie said, "I'll have somebody drive you to the airport."

"It's nice to know you can't live without me."

"Did I make any promises to you? We're square right now aren't we, if you want to take off? Do I owe you anything?"

"The businessman."

"Right, a deal. Have I said it was anything else?"

"You've never said what it was."

"You're a cute kid, Nancy," Ray Ritchie told her. "If I had to replace you, it would probably take me a week."

She remained on the couch after he had gone, aware of the afternoon stillness and aware of herself alone. She sat quietly while Ray and his group whipped off to Chicago to attend the dumb meeting or look at the dumb plant and make big important decisions about their dumb business.

Wow. And she sat here waiting for him.

He would call tomorrow, sometime in the afternoon, and show up about seven with one or two of his group. She would broil steaks as they continued making big important observations and decisions until about eleven. Then she and Ray would be alone and the corporate executive turned lover would say something unbelievable like, "Come here, doll. Miss me?" God. And the big passion scene would get under way. She would give him a look with her hair slanted across one eye, then go around turning off lights and taking glasses into the kitchen and by the time she got to the bedroom, he would be waiting with his one-button Italian-cut suit on the floor, his stomach sucked in, and Scotch and Lea & Perrins on his breath.

Unbelievable.

And he can replace you in a week, she thought. Did you know that?

Okay. She could pack her clothes right now and walk out.

She could smash the lamps, the glasses, and the dishes and then walk out.

She could have Ivory Brothers come in the morning and move out all the furniture and put it in storage.

But she didn't. She got up and turned the radio on and started thinking about the beach house, wondering if she would like it and if there would be enough to do. After a year with Ray Ritchie the severence pay would have to be more than furniture and a few clothes. You bet your ass it would, Raymond.

During the first part of June she was content to lie in the sun by the pool and work on her tan; but by the end of the month there had to be more to do than lie around or play house with Ray when he came up.

The target pistol was fun for about a week. It was a long-barreled .22 Woodsman she had bought in Florida because she liked the look of it or just to have, to *know* she had a gun; maybe that was it. Her first target was the window of a grocery store way out the Shore Road. She would remember driving by in the early evening, then turning around and coming back about forty miles an hour, seeing it on the left side of the road, closed but with a light on, coming up on it and holding the gun extended in her left hand, arm resting on the door sill, not sighting but pointing in the general direction. She fired three times and heard the plate glass shatter as she sailed past, flooring the accelerator to get out of there. The game was to see if she could knock out a window without really aiming, with the right or left hand, at cottages, storefronts, signs, going by at speeds up to seventy: a shooting gallery in reverse. She had tried boats, firing at them from the trees or vacant frontage, but the boats were usually too far out and it was hard to tell when she scored a hit. Officially Nancy went shooting only four times in June, but it was enough to make front-page "Phantom Sniper" stories, with pictures of broken windows, in the Geneva Beach and Holden papers. She looked through the Detroit papers but never found a single mention.

Once she had almost told Bob Jr. about it but at the last moment decided not to. He wouldn't have got it. He would have frowned and said something dumb. It had been fun though, in the beginning, turning him on.

While Bob Jr. worked on the new stairway down to the beach, putting in the support posts and nailing on the side rails and steps, Nancy sunbathed on the beach. It took him a week, though she was sure he could have finished the job in a few days. Nancy would lie on a straw mat in her faded light blue bikini and every once in a while look up at him: Bob Rogers Jr. bare to the waist with his cowboy hat and his apron full of nails. His body was dark reddish brown and the hair on his chest and arms glistened in the sun. He wasn't bad-looking at all, very animal, though his stomach was beginning to hang over his belt and in a few years he'd be a slob.

The afternoon of the third day Nancy didn't go down to the beach. But about three o'clock she stood on the crest of the slope with a bottle of beer in one hand and a good crystal glass in the other, standing in sort of a slouch with her legs apart. He came up and they went over by the pool while he drank the beer and they talked. Nancy fooling around drawing things with her toe and then looking up at him and smiling, once almost losing her balance on the edge of the pool and reaching out to grab his arm and feeling him tighten his muscle. The jerk. He smoked two cigarettes and took little sips of the beer, making it last.

Bob Jr. was wearing a clean sport shirt when he came back the next afternoon. He had mislaid his level and wondered if he'd left it here.

After a trip down and up the stairs, acting it out, looking over the rail along the slope, he said, nope, it must be in the truck and he just didn't see it. But since he was here would she like to go for a ride or something?

"Where?" Nancy asked.

"I don't know. Down the beach."

"Why not stay here?" Nancy said and added, looking up at him with the bedroom brown eyes, "No one's home."

"You talked me into it." Bob Jr. grinned.

She wasn't sure at this point what she wanted him to do. Still, she brought him along, serving him beer on the patio and giving him the basic treatment: the down-under look with dark hair slanting across one eye, putting her foot on the edge of his chair near his leg, leaning over to fool with her sandal strap and letting him look down the front of her blouse. He was on his third beer when he happened to say something about his kids. Why hadn't she thought of it before? Of course he was married; thirty-two or three, living in Geneva Beach all his life, what else would he do?

"Is your wife from Geneva Beach?"

"No, she's a Holden girl."

"But you went to school together."

"Yeah, how did you know?"

"And you've been married about—ten years?"

"Nine."

"Let's see, three children."

"Two, a boy eight and a boy six."

"Are you their big buddy? Take them fishing and camping?"

"We go out, well, once in a while. I got this boat a couple years ago, eighteen footer with a big ninety-five-horse Merc on it."

"Sounds like fun."

"We can go way out with it. I mean way out."

"And do what?"

"Fish. Whatever you want." He was staring at her. "I'll have to take you out sometime." Bob Jr. said.

"When?" Nancy asked. Like that, nailing it down.

After the first time, when he had to come in close because she didn't know his boat, Nancy swam from the beach and Bob Jr. let the boat drift in to meet her, watching her nice easy strokes, then pulled her glistening out of the water, his stomach tightening and his shoulder muscles popping out.

Then heading out full throttle, Bob Jr. sat sideways at the wheel under the canvas top and Nancy stretched out in a plastic chair back in the deckwell by the 95-horse Merc, giving him something to think about when he was home with his wife from Holden and the boy eight and the boy six.

The third time out she gave him something to think about the rest of his life. While he was looking forward, watching the bow take the lake swells, Nancy took off the bra of her bikini and sat back again closing her eyes.

She would love to see his reaction when he looked around, but that wasn't the way to do it. This was the way: eyes closed, very casual, a kind of natural innocence. Finally the motor was shut off and she could feel the boat drifting and his weight on the deck.

"Boy, you take a sunbath, you like to get it all over."

She opened her eyes. "Uh-huh."

"I've heard about topless suits—but, man."

He was standing over her and now eased down to one knee and rested an arm on her chair. "You don't realize how tan a person is," he said, "till you see the difference, huh?"

"I'd like to be tan all over by the end of the summer."

"Well, listen, go ahead. Nobody's going to see you out here."

"I don't think I could."

"Come on, who's going to see you?"

"You would."

"Me? Hell, you think I haven't seen a girl without any clothes on before?"

"Sure," Nancy said. "Your wife."

Bob Jr. laughed. "Some besides her even. Hey, come on." Serious again.

"Please," Nancy said. "Let me get to know you a little better." She smiled, almost shyly. She closed her eyes, leaning back and resting her head on the aluminum frame, giving him a good profile from nose to navel.

42

After a minute passed, she knew he wasn't going to grab her. He wasn't going to risk it. He had something here that had never been within his reach before and he wasn't going to blow it by grabbing her the first time out.

They swam off the boat for a while and on the way back in Bob Jr. said why didn't they do it again tomorrow? Nancy said she was sorry, she was expecting Ray to call. She avoided him the next few days, watching from the bluff as the boat came nosing in out of the deep water, then stepping back out of sight as he lowered the revs and rumbled close to shore.

The following week she pulled up next to his pickup at a Geneva Beach stoplight, seeing his vacant expression crack open into a big dumb grin as he looked her way and leaned out the window.

"Hey! Where you been, stranger?"

Going out the next day, Bob Jr. was relaxed and smiling, smoking one cigarette after another as he pointed out cloud formations and identified landmarks along the shore and commented on how nice the boat was handling.

"You know," he said finally, cutting the motor, "I don't think I ever met a girl like you before."

"Maybe it's just a feeling," Nancy said.

"Sure it's a feeling, a pretty good one."

"Maybe I understand you better than your wife does." She thought: And *he* says—

"You know, it's funny you should say that."

"I've never met a man quite like you before," Nancy said.

Bob Jr. drew on his cigarette and flicked it over the side, way out, then looked at her again.

"You going to take your top off?"

"Not today."

"What do you mean not today?"

"It's too cold."

"Too cold! For Christ sake, it's eighty-nine degrees out!"

"I don't know," Nancy said. "I must have a chill or something. Do you have a sweater?"

He didn't say much on the way in. He kept looking at her sitting back there with her legs tucked beneath her

43

and his sweatshirt down over her knees. She would smile at him every once in a while, letting him know that if he wanted her badly enough, it was going to take more than a boat ride, buddy.

Now, while Bob Jr. was still trying to find out what exactly it would take, Nancy had shifted her interest.

She had a clear mental picture of Ryan standing by Ray's car showing her his muscle. She had met a few Jack Ryans before, in Florida, and she could see him at the dresser combing his hair, looking at himself in the mirror, or in the kitchen opening a can of beer: dark brown and stringy hard above and below the tan lines, thin and slow-moving, a poser.

But there was more to him than that, more to him than the posing and the police record—the resisting arrest and breaking and entering and what he did to the crew leader. Nancy had a feeling about Ryan. Not an emotional feeling, a girl-boy feeling, but a clearly focused zeroed-in feeling, a seeing-him-and-knowing-right-away feeling that Jack Ryan, or someone just like him, was the answer: her way out of here with a lot more than furniture and a few clothes.

The idea had come to her suddenly right after seeing him at the migrant camp. The idea was wild, so far out she had only smiled at first, thinking of what it would do to Ray Ritchie. But the more she thought of the idea, the more she liked it. It was fantastic, way out, and beyond anything she had ever done before. The trouble was, the whole thing would depend on Ryan. It would depend first on whether or not he was staying around Geneva Beach instead of going home, and second, it would depend on his nerve. She had a feeling that if he really wanted to stay, if he had a good reason to stay, he would.

If he didn't have a reason to stay, she might have to give him one. Which shouldn't be too hard. Then play with him to see what he was really like.

But the whole deal, staying and going along with her idea, both, depended really on how much nerve he had.

Which she would have to find out.

FIVE

"HEY, YOU GOT TIME TO HAVE ONE WITH
me?" Mr. Majestyk was swiveled around, heavy legs
apart, his heels hooked in the rungs of the bar stool.

Ryan had noticed him, three stools away: the guy
looked like an ex-pro guard hunched over the bar, leaning on his stubby arms and a dead cigar in the ashtray.
He had been talking to the bartender about fishing, how
the perch must have all been asleep today, and Ryan had
listened because they were close and he could hear them.
He was going to have another beer, so if the guy wanted
to buy, it was okay. He could leave anytime he wanted.
The guy moved over and it was funny how they got to
talking right away: Mr. Majestyk mentioning the picture
in the newspaper, Ryan with the baseball bat, and saying
how he had recognized Luis Camacho.

"Sure, I see that spig before," Mr. Majestyk said.

He had kicked Camacho and a girl spik off his private
beach about two weeks before. "People walk by, that's all
right, along the water. But this guy spread out a blanket
and him and the girl are laying there on private property.
I tell him nice he's got to leave, this is private property.
And he gets abusive. Christ, you should hear the language.
You've heard it, but I mean in front of the people staying
at my place. I want to deck the son of a bitch, but how
does that look? What kind of a place is this, the owner
gets in a fight? You have to handle it better than that."

"What have you got?" Ryan asked. "Cabins?"

"Cabins? The Bay Vista out on the Shore Road." Like,
what's the matter with you? Cabins. "We got fourteen cabana units with two bedrooms, bath, living room and
kitchenette, all with a screen porch, and seven motel

units. We also got a swimming pool, shuffleboard, and play area for the kids."

"So what'd you do about Camacho?"

"Well, the girl, she's nervous as a whore in church and says something to him and they leave. But walking away, he turns and sticks his finger up in the air, you know, like this is what you can do, buddy. I almost took after him."

"He was begging for it," Ryan said. "If it wasn't me, it would've been somebody else."

"That's what I thought," Mr. Majestyk said. "You got time for another?"

"I guess so."

"How about at a table? We can stretch out more."

Ryan went along. It was nice here. There was a smell of beer in the place, but it was not a small-town tavern or a shot and a beer kind of bar. It was a beach bar, a marina bar, with a fishnet and life preservers and brass fixtures on white walls and a good view of the boat docks. It was quiet but not too quiet. There was record music and people were talking, having a good time, nobody dressed up: people who'd been out in their boats and stopped off for a couple. It was a nice place. He had spotted the waitress right away and that was nice too: blond ponytail and tight red pants. She had passed close to him going to the service section of the bar, where there were curved chrome handles like the top of a swimming pool ladder.

Then at the table with a pitcher of Michelob and a couple of bags of Fritos and some beer nuts: Mr. Majestyk asking questions about Camacho and what kind of a crew leader he was—saying spig for spik and hid for hit, like "when you hid the son of a bitch"—talking easily but talking a lot.

Then he didn't say anything for maybe a minute. Ryan looked around and sipped his beer and finally Mr. Majestyk said, "Listen, do you want me to tell you something?"

"Go ahead."

"Sitting at the bar, I wasn't going to say anything to you. And then I figured what the hell."

"Yeah?"

46

"Do you know they got a movie of you belting the guy?"

"I heard about it."

"I saw it the other day. Three times."

Ryan was looking at him now. "What'd they show it to you for?"

"Well, if they hadn't dropped the charge and you came to trial? It would've been in my court." Mr. Majestyk paused. "I'm the J.P. here, justice of the peace."

Ryan kept his eyes on him.

"I'm telling you why I saw the movies, that's all."

"What's the beer for?"

"I'm on the Chamber of Commerce."

Ryan didn't smile. "I got to get going."

"Buddy, if you're nervous about it, maybe you'd better."

"I'm not nervous about anything." Ryan sipped his beer.

"But they told you you had to leave." Mr. Majestyk waited, letting him relax a little. "There's no charge against you. How can they make you leave if you want to stay?"

"They phony something up. Vagrancy or something."

"You got money?"

Ryan looked at him. "Enough."

"So how can you be arrested for vagrancy? You ever been picked up for that?"

"No."

"They said something about you were arrested a couple of times. Car theft?"

"Joyriding. Suspended."

"What about this resisting arrest?"

"A guy was giving me a hard time. I hit him."

"The cop?"

"No, before."

"With what?"

"I hit him with a beer bottle."

"Broken one?"

"No, this guy tried to pull something. I didn't get arrested for hitting him. It was after, when the cop told me to drop the bottle."

47

"You didn't drop it quick enough."

Ryan was looking at the waitress. She had the masked look a lot of waitresses put on, telling nothing, letting you know you weren't anything special. Probably a stuck-up broad who was dumb and didn't know it. Broads like that burned him up. She looked nice, though: starched ruffled blouse and the tight red pants, like a swordfighter outfit. She came over with another pitcher of beer. He watched Mr. Majestyk give her tail a little pat and she didn't seem to mind.

"What's your name, honey?" His big hand resting gently on her red hip.

"Mary Jane."

"Mary Jane, I want you to meet Jack Ryan."

"I've seen him before," she said, looking at Ryan as she placed the pitcher on the table. He saw her eyes and it gave him a funny feeling. She had seen him before. She knew about him. She had decided things about him. He watched her turn to the bar again, the nice tight shape of the red pants.

"Some guys I'd like to have taken and used a beer bottle on," Mr. Majestyk said, "I had a tavern in Detroit—oh, fifteen years ago now. These guys would come off the shift from Dodge Main. They come in, every one of them, a shot and a beer. Set them right down the bar, every stool, then go back and pour another shot right down the bar again."

Ryan's gaze followed the waitress. A nice little black ribbon tied around the ponytail. Nice, the black with the blond hair.

"Then go back," Mr. Majestyk said, "boom boom boom, pick up the dough. The third time just hit the guys that want another. This guy I don't know is there one time and he says, 'God *damn,* how do you remember what everybody's drinking?' Amazed. I just shrug like it's nothing. Every Polack in the place is drinking Seven Crown and Strohs. Sixty-five cents."

Ryan left his canvas bag at the bar and they went to a restaurant over on the main street for dinner, Estelle's: a counter and booths with formica tops and place mats that illustrated Michigan as "The Water-Winter Wonderland."

48

They ordered steaks with American fries after Ryan bet they wouldn't have boiled potatoes and they didn't.

Mr. Majestyk stared at him, hunched over with his arms on the table edge. "You like boiled potatoes?"

"Boiled potatoes, just plain or with some parsley," Ryan said. "It's like a real potato. I mean it's got the most potato taste."

"Right!" Mr Majestyk said, with a tone that said it was the correct answer.

"When I was at home," Ryan said, "on Sunday my mother would have veal roast or pork roast and boiled potatoes. Not mashed or fried or anything. Boiled. You'd take two or three potatoes and cut them up so they covered about half the plate? Then pour gravy all over it. But try and get a boiled potato in a restaurant."

"Where did you live in Detroit?"

"Highland Park. Just north of where Ford Tractor was. Up by Sears."

"I know where it is. Your father work at Ford's?"

"He worked for the DSR, but he's dead now. He died when I was thirteen."

"I had some friends worked for the DSR. Hell, they started when they still had streetcars. All retired now or doing something else."

"I don't think my dad ever ran a streetcar. What I remember, he drove a Woodward bus. It'd say RIVER going downtown, you know? And FAIRGROUNDS coming back."

"Sure I've ridden it."

They didn't talk much eating the steaks and fries. Ryan pictured the Sunday dinners again in the dining room that was also his bedroom: his mother and his two older sisters and most of the time one or the other's boyfriend; his dad not always there, not if he had to work Sunday. It was a two-bedroom apartment on the fourth floor, the top floor, of an old building; his mother and dad in one bedroom, the two sisters in the other one, which was always messed up with clothes and magazines and curlers and crap. He slept in the dining room on a studio couch with maple arms and kept his shirts, socks, and underwear in the bottom drawer of the secretary in the living room. He'd be sitting there at the dining room table doing his homework hearing the television in the living room, and his dad would come in carrying his changer, his blue-gray DSR hat on the side of his head and crushed in like a World War II fighter pilot's hat. If he had stopped for a drink, just a couple, you could tell it. On his day off his dad would sit at the dining room table with a clean sport shirt on, his hair combed and his shoes shined, and play solitaire. He would play it most of the day, with a cigarette in the corner of his mouth, his head raised and his eyes looking down half closed. In the afternoon he would drink beer and read the paper. The paper was the only thing he read.

"You want some A-one?"

"No, just ketchup."

His dad never looked like a bus driver. He was nice-looking. Dark hair. Sort of a slick guy. Good dresser. But he was a bus driver in his forties, making about a hundred and a quarter a week with a wife and three children and living in an apartment building with kitchen smells and peeling plaster out in the hall. He could crush in his hat and wear it hotshot on the side of his head and pretend he was piloting a 707 or a truckload of explosives up the Alcan, but it was still a DSR bus and there was no way to make it something else.

"How about dessert?"

"I don't think so." Ryan sipped his water. "You know, my dad died when he was forty-six."

"Well"—Mr. Majestyk was looking at his hand on his water glass and now Ryan's eyes dropped to the hand, a thick, toughened hand with swollen knuckles and cracked, yellowed nails, a hand that made the heavy restaurant tumbler seem thin and fragile—"I don't know. I guess a person just dies."

"Yeah, I guess we all have to die."

"I don't mean that," Mr. Majestyk said. "I don't mean it that way. I mean we're *supposed* to die. You can't kill yourself, but that's what we're here for, to die. Are you a Catholic? With your name, I mean——"

"Yeah. I was."

"Well, don't you know what I mean?"

"I never was an altar boy or anything."

"You don't have to be an altar boy, for Christ sake. You were taught, weren't you? You went to church."

"Let's not get into all that."

Mr. Majestyk's serious gaze held, then began to relax, and he smiled with his perfect-looking false teeth. "What're we talking about dying for. Come on, let's go over the Pier."

He didn't see the waitress in the red pants. She was gone and a dumpy Indian-looking waitress was serving the tables. There were girls scattered around the place, but none of them seemed to be alone. There was more noise, the lights were on and there were a lot more people now. There was a long table of beer-drinking college-looking Hermans who had probably been out sailing or cruising around in their cruisers and were loud and never shut up. It wasn't as good as before.

When they were at a table again with a pitcher of beer, he saw Bob Jr. come in with the girl. He didn't recognize the girl right away because he was watching Bob Jr. as they moved through the people down to the end of the bar. Bob Jr. was all slicked up in a real slick checkered sport shirt with the collar tips pointing out to his shoulders, short sleeves turned up once, silver expando watchband and everything, big can hanging over the bar stool now and his hair combed back like Roy Rogers. The girl with him went on to the ladies room.

"You get these guys from Dodge Main off the shift," Mr. Majestyk was saying. "But get them in at night, that's the trick."

Bob Jr. looked this way, toward the front end of the bar, and, sure enough, his forehead was pure white.

"Well, it was August, so we figure how about fresh corn? All you can eat for fifty cents with this sign out in front. Now we only have one pot," Mr. Majestyk was saying. "On purpose. One that would hold maybe a dozen and a half ears. So the guys come in and order the corn; they're going to see how much they can eat, see? Fifty cents, you can't beat it. But they got to wait because only with the one pot we can't cook more'n a dozen and a half ears. So while they wait they're drinking, I mean throwing

51

it down. We make money on the booze and, listen, we make money on the *corn*. Because, see, we get it for twenty-five cents a dozen out by Pontiac and these guys, they pay fifty cents, right?" Mr. Majestyk sat back, the winner. "But none of them eat more than twelve, four-teen ears apiece!"

Ryan smiled and laughed a little bit, but he wasn't pic-turing any Polacks eating corn; he was watching the dark-haired girl coming back from the ladies room, rec-ognizing her and suddenly having a funny feeling shoot through him from his scalp right down to his hind end.

Ryan let the smile fade and said, "You know Bob Rogers, works for Ritchie?"

With a heavy knuckle Mr. Majestyk was wiping the moisture from his eye. "Bob Junior? Sure, his old man and I play pinochle."

"He's down at the end of the bar."

Mr. Majestyk glanced around. "Yeah, I see him."

"Who's the girl with him?"

Now Mr. Majestyk straightened and looked over his shoulder again. He came back slowly, gazing around, so no one would think he was staring. He took a sip of beer. "That little lady's in some trouble."

"Who is she?"

"I forget her name. Nancy something. She's supposed to be like a secretary to Ritchie, but that's a bunch of crap."

"He keeps her here?"

"That's the word, buddy. He keeps her."

"Whereabouts?"

"In this place he's got on the beach. His wife comes up, he moves the broad over to his hunting place up by the farm."

"She looks young."

"How old do you have to be?"

"I mean for him. Ritchie."

"Ask him—how should I know?"

"What's she doing with Bob Junior?"

Mr Majestyk glanced around again. "That dumb bas-tard. He's got a good job, a nice family, a speedboat. His old man leases all the cucumber land to Ritchie Food and all Bob Junior's got to do is work the crews——"

"He's a horse's ass."

Mr. Majestyk shrugged, making a face. "He's all right, he's a big kid. He thinks he's the Lone goddamn Ranger or something."

"You said the girl was in some trouble."

"Reckless driving. She's got to appear in my court sometime next month."

"What's so bad about that?"

Mr. Majestyk leaned over the table on his forearms. "I'm not talking about running a red light. She almost killed a couple of kids."

"You know it was her fault?"

"All right. These two Geneva boys are out in their car, a piece of junk just riding around looking to raise some hell, you know, or somebody to race. They spot the broad cruising along in her Mustang, so naturally they pull up alongside and start giving her the business, making remarks, asking her if she wants to race or go in the bushes, I don't know."

"So what happened?"

"Well, they don't get a rise out of her, so they pass and go on wherever they're going. But a couple of miles later they've turned off the Shore Road and they're on this county road, gravel, and they see these lights coming up behind them. They expect the car to pass, but the car doesn't pass, it bangs into their rear end. They don't know what's coming off. They speed up and the car—it's the broad—gets right on their bumper and guns it. These guys they try to go faster, they try to shake her off, you know, swerving, but she hangs on and now she's pushing them sixty, seventy miles an hour."

"Yeah?"

"They try to brake and they burn the linings right off. They can't do anything, this crazy broad keeps pushing, gunning it, and she's going a good seventy—they both swear to it—when she backs off. She must have seen it: the road dead-ends at a crossroad and beyond is this plowed field. Well, these guys try to swerve, they fly over

53

the ditch and hit the plowed field and roll over three times."

"What happened to the guys?"

"One of them's okay, a few cuts. The other kid's got two broken legs and some internal injuries."

"How'd they know it was her?"

"They saw her, for Christ sake."

"I mean they could be lying."

"Yeah, with her front end all banged the hell in."

Nancy said, "I thought you told him to leave."

"Who?"

She brushed the hair from her eye, nodding toward Ryan's table. "The one today. You know."

"Son of a gun. I don't believe it," Bob Jr. said.

As Bob Jr. looked around, his broad back, the checkered shirt tight across his shoulders, was close to her and she rested her hand lightly on his arm.

"He's taking his time about it, isn't he?" the girl said.

"He's taking more'n I gave him."

"Maybe he's decided to stay."

"He'll leave if I got to run him down the highway with a stick."

"Maybe he's not afraid of you." She ran her hand up his arm to the shoulder. "Look what he did to the Mexican."

"He doesn't have to be afraid," Bob Jr. said. "Just have some sense."

"Are you going to talk to him?"

"If he isn't out of here before we leave."

"I'm ready anytime," Nancy said.

Mr. Majestyk was studying his glass. He said, "Listen, what I was thinking—what if you came to work at the Bay Vista?" He looked up at Ryan, as if surprised at what he had said. "Hey, what about it? Forty bucks a week—no, I'll pay you fifty, also you get room and board; nice room you can fix up."

"Doing what?"

"Anything needs to be done. Painting, taking care of the beach, repairs. I got this arthritis in my hands. See them knuckles?"

"For the rest of the summer?"

"Rest of the summer, maybe longer. I'm thinking of staying open for hunting season. Get these guys up from Detroit, give them nice rooms, feed them. You ever cook any?"

"I worked in a place once. Like a White Tower, only bigger."

"You cook, huh?"

"Fry chef."

"After hunting season, I don't know. If we had good hills for the skiers, but that's all up by Petoskey."

"Who's there, just you and your wife?"

"She's been dead two years. But my daughter, she lives in Warren, comes up a couple times a year with the kids. Ronnie and Gayle—boy, those kids. It was my daughter fixed the place up for me, you know, picked out the drapes and the studio couches and all the pictures, everything."

"Yeah, well I don't know." The girl with Bob Jr., Nancy, was looking at him again and it gave him a funny feeling, as if, like the waitress in the red pants, she knew all about him. More than he knew about her. He watched her slide off the bar stool and he watched Bob Jr. stand up and look right at him.

Mr. Majestyk leaned into the table. "Do you want me to tell you something?"

"Just a second. I think we got company." Mr. Majestyk straightened and looked up as Bob Jr., coming first, edging past the people at the bar, reached the table. The girl stood by the bar, waiting for him.

"What're you trying to pull?" Bob Jr. said to Ryan. "Are you trying to get cute with me?"

"Jesus Christ," Mr. Majestyk said. "Who would want to get cute with you?"

"Hi, Walter." Bob Jr. was serious. He didn't smile.

"Hey, where's your Lone Ranger hat?"

"Walter, you mind if I have a word with this guy?"

"Let me see," Mr. Majestyk said. "Yes, I think I would."

Bob Jr. was looking at Ryan, not listening to Majestyk.

"You know what I told you this morning. I said at the time I wasn't going to tell you again."

"Then, what are you telling him for?" Mr. Majestyk asked.

Bob Jr. said to Ryan, "We better step outside a minute."

Mr. Majestyk moved his hand across the table toward Ryan. "Stay where you are."

"Walter, this is company business."

"What company? Does he work for your company?"

"We paid him off and he agreed to leave," Bob Jr. said. "On the strength of that agreement, I'm going to see he lives up to his end."

"Hey, Bob," Mr. Majestyk said, "don't give me any agreement crap, all right? You paid him because you owed him the dough. Now he don't work for you anymore and there isn't anything you can do to make him leave if he don't want to."

"Walter, you're a friend of my dad's and all, but this is between me and him."

Ryan finished the beer in his glass and poured it full again. He was keeping a good hold, but it was almost too much, and it would be easy to let go, Bob Jr. standing close to the table with his hands on his hips and his big silver cowboy belt buckle shining level with his eyes.

Ryan said, not looking up, "Why don't you quit standing there? Why don't you and your friend sit down and have a beer?"

Mr. Majestyk smiled. "Now, that's a nice suggestion. Bob, what do you say? It's early."

"We've had ours. We're leaving now and I expect this fella's leaving the same time we are."

Ryan looked up at him. He said, "Don't press it, all right? Not anymore."

"Listen, boy, if I didn't have somebody with me, I'd pick you up and carry you out."

"No you wouldn't," Ryan said.

Mr. Majestyk was watching him. His gaze shifted to Bob Jr. and he said, not hurrying it but before Bob Jr. could say anything, "I invited this guy to have a beer with me. I'm not through yet and he's not through. Maybe we'll have a couple more pitchers, maybe we'll have ten more. I don't know. But what I want to know is if you're going to stand there until we're finished."

"Walter, I told this guy this morning what he had to do."

"Fine, you told him. Now, Bob, either sit down or stand someplace else, all right?"

"You're saying I'm butting in. Walter, I'm saying this guy and I have business."

"Let's say we're both right," Mr. Majestyk said, "and neither of us will give in to the other. Meanwhile you left that nice-looking young lady standing by herself. Is that nice, Bob? What would your father say? What would your wife say?"

Bob Jr. hesitated long enough to show them he wasn't being forced into anything he didn't want to do. And when enough time had passed, looking at Ryan and slowly moving his gaze to Mr. Majestyk, he said, "I'll run her home, but don't be surprised if you see me again." He had to give Ryan another look before turning away.

The girl waited with her arms folded, watching Ryan, then looking up at Bob Jr.'s tight, serious expression as he came toward her. She said, "Wow," and walked out ahead of him.

"Do you want to know something?" Mr. Majestyk said. His eyes were a little watery; he was feeling the beer, but he spoke quietly, well enough controlled. "You probably wonder why I want to hire you. Why you. Do you want me to tell you why?"

"Go ahead," Ryan said. The guy was going to tell him anyway.

"This might sound nuts, I don't know, but I saw the movies, right? And I talked to the sheriff's cops about you and I said to myself, 'That's a good kid. He stands up. Maybe he's had a rough life, bummed around, and had to work. No chance to go to college, no trade—' You don't have a trade, do you?"

"Not that pays anything."

"Right," Mr Majestyk said. "No college education, no trade. I think to myself, 'What's he going to do? He's a good one. He's got something other guys don't have. The son of a bitch stands up. But listen, I know this. It isn't easy always to keep standing up. I mean, it's better if you got somebody to help you once in a while. You understand what I mean?"

Just picturing the girl standing there, waiting by the bar, and the way she looked at him before she walked out, gave him the funny feeling again.

"Do you understand what I mean?"

"Yeah, I understand."

"So I said to myself, 'Do you want to see him throw his life away, bumming around, getting into trouble, or you going to help him? Give him an opportunity, a place to live, something to do.' "

"That's what you said to yourself."

"Maybe not in those words."

"I go to work at the Bay Vista."

"Say till Labor Day, then we see what happens."

"Janitor at a motel."

"Not a janitor."

"Handyman. I become your handyman and I'm all set."

"Listen, I'm not giving you anything. You come to work for me you work. Maybe I find out you're a bum and I got to throw you out."

"If I take the job."

"If you take the job, right."

"You going to protect me from Bob Junior too? See nothing happens to me?"

Mr. Majestyk stared at him. He did not move or show anything in his eyes, though a line seemed to tighten down the sides of his nose. He sat hunched forward, not taking his eyes from Ryan, and finally he said, "You can stand up, but Jesus Christ you're dumb, aren't you?"

"I never asked you to stick up for me."

"Forget it." Mr. Majestyk said. "All right?" He said it quietly, his expression dead. "I'm going home. Come with me or stay, I don't care. If you feel like it, think over what I said and if you want to work, come by my place tomorrow morning eight o'clock. If you don't want to, don't. Either way you'll do what you want."

He went to the bar to settle their bill and walked out without looking back.

"What's the matter?" the Indian-looking waitress said to Ryan. "Doesn't he feel good?"

"He went home, that's all."

"He said you could have whatever you wanted."

Ryan looked at her. "I never asked him for anything."

"Who said you did?" The Indian-looking waitress took away the empty pitcher and glasses. A few minutes later she watched Ryan pick up his bag and walk out.

SIX

THE PICTURE WINDOW OF CABANA NO. 5

looked out on the shallow end of the swimming pool, a deserted pool at nine in the morning, partly in shade, unmoving.

Virginia Murray had been up since a quarter to seven. She had eaten breakfast: orange juice, toast, and Sanka, straightened the kitchenette, made her bed, showered, removed the curlers from her hair and combed it out, and had put on her aqua bathing suit and terry-cloth robe. She had also written to her mother and father, telling them, oh, was it ever good not to have to get up and rush to work. She didn't mind at all now the other girls not coming. It was more of a rest being alone.

Sitting on the couch across from the picture window, and with the floral print draperies drawn open, she could look straight out to the swimming pool and the cabanas across the way and see it all framed as a scene, a stage set, while she remained in the darkness of the audience. She thumbed through *McCall's*. She looked at her watch: a little after nine. She pulled at the bra of her one-piece aqua bathing suit where the edge dug into her chest. She looked in the straw bag next to her to make sure the Coppertone was inside. And the Kleenex. And comb, which she took out of the straw bag now and went into the bathroom and combed her hair again in the mirror, her head turned, cocked slightly, the corner of one eye watching the movement of the comb, the eye now and again meeting the eye in the mirror and looking away. She returned to the couch and sat on the towel she had spread over an end section. As she picked up *McCalls* again she saw two little boys standing at the edge of the pool.

The Fisher boys from No. 14, one of the cabanas facing the beach. In a few minutes their teen-age sister would come to watch them; then the father would come and later on, about eleven, the mother. By that time most of the Bay Vista people would have appeared: the children first, the children suddenly everywhere, the adults coming out gradually, saying good morning and carefully choosing lounge chairs, moving them closer together or farther apart, turning them to face the swimming pool or the sun or away from the sun.

The Fishers would come to the pool.

The couple on their honeymoon would come to the pool. From No. 10, the cabana directly across from Virginia Murray's.

The family with the little dark-haired children, probably Italian, would come to the pool and the mother would talk to Mrs. Fisher, the two women with heavy legs and beach coats and straw hats with ornaments in the bands that looked like pine cones.

The people in No. 1 would stay on their lawn at the umbrella table and from the shade watch their children on the beach.

The two young couples in No. 11—without children or away from them—who were building a wall of empty beer cans along the railing of their screened porch (Virginia Murray had counted and estimated over 100 cans by Sunday evening) would do down to the beach at ten; one of the men would come up for the Scotch-Kooler of beer just before noon; they would all come up for lunch at one, return to the beach at two, and begin drinking beer again at four, at ease, the men saying funny things and all four of them laughing.

The woman in No. 9, the redhead who wore makeup to the pool, would come out with her little girl about eleven, though the little girl would have come out several times before to watch the other children. Sometimes the little girl would beg to go down to the beach and play in the sand, but her mother would tell her, Cheryl Ann, it was too sunny today.

There were other people at the Bay Vista, in the cabanas and in the motel units facing the Beach Road, who would be at the swimming pool sometimes and at the beach sometimes. Virginia Murray recognized most of them, but she had not labeled them or decided anything about them.

There was Mr. Majestyk, too. He seemed nice. Friendly in a brusk, uneducated sort of way; walking around in his undershirt—always the undershirt and a baseball cap—always going somewhere to fix something or moving the diving raft farther out or driving his bulldozer around the beach.

And since yesterday morning, Jack Ryan.

There was no doubt in Virginia Murray's mind now; he was the one in the newspaper picture with the baseball bat. It was amazing that she still had the paper, over a week old, and yesterday, wrapping her grapefruit rind in the paper, seeing him in the picture and then seeing him here. She had watched him all yesterday afternoon; the same one all right.

She sat on the couch in her aqua bathing suit, gazing out the picture window of No. 5, waiting for the day's activity to begin and trying to think of who Jack Ryan reminded her of. Sort of the type who'd wear a black leather jacket. Sort of. But he wasn't dirty or greasy-looking. It was the way he stood. Like a bullfighter. That was it—like the one on the poster in their rec room at home: *Plaza de Toros de Linares* and below it the bullfighter standing with his feet together, his back arched and his cheeks sucked in, looking down his chest at the bull twisted around his body.

She had not seen him speak to anyone but Mr. Majestyk and she wondered what it would be like to talk to him, though she knew they had nothing in common; he wasn't her type. She pictured herself alone in Cabana 5. Late at night. She saw herself reading in bed, then turning off the light and lying in the dark. It wouldn't happen right away. But after a few minutes she would hear the sound, the scratching sound—no, more of a creaking sound—the screen door opening. She would lie in the dark with her eyes open and hear someone moving about the front room. She would hear him in the hall, then see his dark shape in the bedroom doorway. She would wait until he was in the room before switching on the light. "Can I help you?" Virginia Murray would ask. It would be Jack Ryan, a kitchen knife in his hand as he came toward the bed.

She would have to think about the next part a little more. It was still not clear exactly what she would say. Her voice would be calm, not soothing really but having the same effect, and her eyes would hold his, showing not fear but understanding. Gradually he would relax. He would put the knife down. He would sit on the edge of the bed. She would ask questions and he would begin to tell her about himself. He would tell her about his past life, his problems, and she would listen calmly, not shocked by anything he said. He would ask her if he could speak to her again and she would touch his arm and smile and say, "Of course. But right now you'd better run off to bed and get a good night's sleep."

Something like that. She pictured the two of them sitting on the beach, but it was a glimpse of a scene. That would be later on. There would be time for that later.

Now, sitting on the couch, she saw him coming out from between No. 10 and 11 carrying the long aluminum pole with the fine net on the end of it. She looked at her watch. Nine twenty.

She watched Jack Ryan dip the net in the water at the deep end and walk the length of the pool with it, skimming the surface to pick up leaves and dead insects. He said something to the two Fisher boys and they grinned at him and jumped into the water, trying to touch the net end of the pole. He moved gradually back to the deep end, intent on what he was doing, his elbows out and his arms rigid, holding the pole: a boatman, not a bullfighter, a dark gondolier with no shirt or shoes or belt—he should have a big wide black belt—and not khaki pants cut off above the knees, some other kind, whatever gondoliers wore. Virginia couldn't remember. It had been four years ago with her mother and father, the year she had graduated from Marygrove College.

When the Fisher's teen-age daughter appeared, walking along the side of the pool, Virginia Murray got up and went into the bedroom. In front of the mirror she tied a kerchief loosely over her hair, the eyes not looking into the eyes in the mirror but aware of the fixed semiexpectant expression of her face. She turned to go out. But now she went to the window next to the bed, unlocked it, and tried to raise it from the bottom. No, it wouldn't budge. It still wouldn't budge. Virginia returned to the front room folded the towel over her arm, picked up the straw bag, and stepped out of No. 5, letting the screen door close gently. Putting on her sunglasses, looking up at the sky and the trees this beautiful morning, she strolled over to the swimming pool.

"Just the bugs and crap," Mr. Majestyk said. "You can vacuum the bottom tomorrow."

"What else?"

"The beach. Rake it up where the kids had the hot dog roast. Maybe you should do that next."

"It doesn't matter to me."

Mr. Majestyk looked at him. "Then the shower head in Number Nine. She says it just drips out. Leaks up in the ball joint."

"I don't know how to fix any shower."

"You clean it out. You take it off and bring it over the shop, I'll show you how to clean it. The tools are in the storage room next to yours."

"What else?"

"I got to check. I'll let you know."

"I haven't had any breakfast yet."

"So get up in the morning. I eat at seven. You want to eat, you eat at seven."

"Thanks a lot."

63

"Don't mention it," Mr. Majestyk said. He walked off between 11 and 12.

Ryan worked a flat, almost empty pack of Camels out of his pants pocket and lighted one with the aluminum pole angled down into the water from under one arm. The first drag tasted awful because he hadn't had any coffee or anything to eat.

He started along the edge again, holding the aluminum pole rigid.

Virginia Murray said, "I wonder if you might have time——"

But he was past her, the pole angled into the water and the net skimming the surface.

She waited for his return pass. Almost to her lounge chair. Now.

"I wonder if you could look at my window?"

"What?"

"I have a window I can't budge. It won't open at all."

"What one are you in?"

"Number Five."

"Okay, I'll look at it."

"It's all right when there's a breeze from the front. I can leave the door open and just lock the screen."

"I'll look at it. Number Five."

"When do you think you could?"

"Well, I'll finish this, then I got another thing."

"Thank you very much." Her eyes dropped to *McCall's* and she turned a page. She had spoken to him.

Ryan circled the pool, around the diving board, and moved down to the shallow end. That was enough bug-catching for one day. He carried the pole across the shuffleboard courts to the equipment storage room in the motel, mounted it on its wall hooks and picked up the toolbox, then cut across to No. 9 and knocked on the door. A little girl came and stood looking up at him through the screen.

"My mother's still asleep."

"I just want to fix the shower."

The place smelled funny; it needed to be swept out and the kitchen cleaned. The little girl's milk and cereal were

64

on the table with an open loaf of bread and open jars of peanut butter and grape jelly.

"You had your breakfast?"

"Uh-huh."

"I haven't had mine yet," Ryan said. "Hey, you know how to make a peanut butter and jelly sandwich?"

"Course."

"Why don't you make me one while I'm fixing the shower?"

The bedroom door was open, but he didn't look in going past it. The bathroom was a mess, sand and dirty towels on the floor, the top of the toilet tank heaped with curlers and cosmetics. He had noticed the redhead yesterday, alone here with her little girl, not bad-looking and built, but now he crossed her off as a possibility. He got the shower head loose with a wrench—easier than he thought it would be—and went back to the living room.

"Hey, that looks good. You're a good sandwich maker."

"My mother taught me," the little girl said.

"It's perfect. Listen, I'm going to take it with me, okay?"

He got out of there. He ate the peanut butter and jelly sandwich on the way over to Mr. Majestyk's, cutting around behind the cabanas, taking his time. The Bay Vista wasn't a bad-looking place: two rows of identical tan-painted cement-block cottages extending to the beach and hidden from the Shore Road by a seven-unit motel. Ryan was in No. 7, the end one behind the office. All of the cottages faced in on the swimming pool or the patio or the shuffleboard courts or the barbeque grilles except No. 1 and No. 14; they looked out over the beach and rented for twenty dollars a week more than the other units.

Mr. Majestyk's tan ranch house was on beach frontage adjacent to No. 1. His beige Dodge station wagon was in the garage next to his light-duty bulldozer with a scoop on the front. Mr. Majestyk was in the breezeway between the house and the garage, in the screened area he used as a workshop.

"Here's the shower thing."

Mr. Majestyk nodded. "You got the beach done?"

"I'm going to do that next."

"I'll show you how to clean this." Mr. Majestyk wiped his hands on a rag and took the shower head. "It's got to be freed up. Clean out all the corrosion and crap."

"Maybe I better do the beach first, you know, before a lot of people get down there."

"Yeah, what if the lady wants to take a shower?"

"I don't think she ever does."

"Who the hell are you?"

"Well, what would she take a shower for now? Ten o'clock in the morning?"

"Go on do the beach. I'll clean it. Listen, we eat at noon or six, depending whether I got to be in court."

"I forgot you're a judge."

"J.P. Today we eat at noon."

Ryan went to the garage and came back. "I don't see the rake."

"It's around by the front."

Ryan moved off again, rounding the corner of Mr. Majestyk's house into sun and evergreen shade, the sun hot on the thermopane picture window, flower beds edged with stones painted white: an Army-post garden except for the birdhouse and the plastic flamingoes feeding beneath it.

He picked up the rake and went down to the beach and started cleaning up, raking the charred wood and wrappers and pop bottles left from the hot dog roast. He'd have to get a box or something. But first he'd work along the beach and make about five or six piles. It was good being in the sun, hot, with a nice breeze every once in a while. He put on his sunglasses and lit a cigarette. There weren't many people around. The beer drinkers from No. 11 were still quiet, not talking yet. The couple from No. 10 were on a blanket, off by themselves. The little kids from No. 1 were playing in the sand and a few boys were fooling around with a plastic baseball and bat.

He watched the ball sail up against the sky in a high arc, an easy one, the kind you camp under that Colavito would punch his glove waiting for; as the ball came down he saw the girl in the bathing suit walking along the edge of the water, a good fifty yards off, but Ryan knew right away who it was: the dark hair and sunglasses, the slim dark girl figure in a yellow two-piece suit that was almost but not quite a bikini: flat brown stomach and the little line of yellow, good legs, thin but good.

She looked this way, brushing her hair aside with the tips of her fingers. She saw him, he was sure; but it didn't mean she recognized him, he could be just a guy raking the beach. Maybe he should wave or move down to the water to meet her, but he decided right away that would be dumb. He let her go by, watching now as she moved away, until she was so small she blended into the shapes and colors far down the beach.

If Ray Ritchie's beach house was in that direction, she was going home. If it was the other way, she'd be back. He thought about her looking at him in the bar and he thought about what Mr. Majestyk had said, about Ray Ritchie keeping her. He had never known a girl who lived with somebody. He knew all kinds of girls, but not one like that. She should have blond hair and great big jugs and be taller and older and wear high heels. And he remembered Mr. Majestyk saying, "How old do they have to be?" He wondered how old she was and where she was from and where she had met Ray Ritchie and how he had got her to live with him, how he had put it when he asked her.

He would say something to her if she came back, but he couldn't think of what to say and began smoothing the sand again with the rake.

Just relax, he told himself. What's the matter with you? It was funny, he knew she was going to come back. It didn't surprise him at all to see her, finally, a spot of yellow in the distance, coming slowly, taking forever, but he still couldn't think of anything. He said in his mind, "Hi, how you doing?" He said, "Well, look who's here." He said, "Hey, where you going?" He said to himself, "For Christ sake, cut it out."

Ryan moved closer to the water and started raking the sand, smoothing it, not looking at the girl but still seeing her, the slim dark legs and long hair:

He timed it right, straightening up when she was only a few yards off, to lean on the rake like a spearman.

She looked at him, then, unhurriedly, away from him. Ryan waited until she was past, so she would have to turn around.

"Hey."

She took two or three more steps before turning half around slowly, legs apart, and looked at him.

"I've been wanting to ask you something," Ryan said. He gave her time to say *what?*

But she didn't. She waited.

And finally Ryan said, "I was wondering what you were looking at me for in the bar?"

She waited a moment longer. "Are you sure I was looking at you?"

Ryan nodded. "I'm sure. You think it's about time we quit fooling around?"

She smiled but barely. "What's the matter with fooling around?" The wind blew her hair and she brushed it from her eye, the hair slanting across her forehead, dark brown and probably brown eyes.

"I mean wasting time," Ryan said.

"I know what you mean."

She was at ease, studying him; he hung onto the rake handle and stared back at her.

"I'm surprised to see you," Nancy said. "Bob Junior doesn't scare you?"

"If I want to stay around here, I guess it's up to me."

"How did you get the job?"

"I don't know. The guy offered it to me."

"For the summer?"

"I don't know. I guess."

"You're not too sure of much, are you?"

He stared at her, waiting for the words, and she stared back at him. He had never had trouble talking to people, especially girls, and the feeling tightened him up. He didn't like it and he thought, What are you being so nice for?

Nancy kept watching him, not smiling or rubbing it in, but watching him. She said, "Do you want to start over?"

"I don't know," Ryan said.

"You could come to my house and play." She raised her arm and pointed. "That way, almost a mile. White stairs and a lamppost at the top."

"I guess Mr. Ritchie's not here."

"Nope."

"Who's there with you? I mean, a maid or something?"

"Nobody."

"Don't you get scared, alone?"

She shook her head, touching her hair again. "I like it."

"What do you do?"

"Different things."

"Like what?"

"Come tonight and find out."

"I don't know."

He watched her shrug and turn away. She was expecting him to say something. He was sure she was waiting for it and that was good. He watched her walk off waiting for it, not able to look back now. They could shake their tail and expect the guy to sit up, but he had done enough sitting up for one day. She'd come by this afternoon or tomorrow, same time, same station. So why get excited? Right?

You're damn right, Ryan thought.

SEVEN

ONCE WHEN JACK RYAN WAS THIRTEEN, he hung from the roof of their apartment building, four stories above the alley, to see if he could do it. The first time he tried it, he didn't hang all the way. He sat down on the edge, in the back of the building where there was no cornice, and rolled over and held on with his chest and forearms, his face close to the dry tar surface of the roof and his legs over the side. He pushed himself up, pressing his hands flat, until he could hook a knee over the edge and the rest was easy. He walked around the roof for a while, taking little breaths and letting his hands hang limp and flexing the fingers, the way a sprinter does before he turns and walks over to his lane and sets himself on the starting block. It was a summer morning and he was alone on the roof, above the round tops of the elms and the peaks of the houses and the chimneys and television antennas. He could hear cars on Woodward Avenue a half black away and a car below him in the alley moving slowly, squeaking, taking a long time to pass the building. When he was ready, he moved to the edge of the roof again and sat down with his legs hanging. He could do it and knew he could do it if he was careful and didn't let himself get scared or do anything dumb. But just knowing he could do it wasn't enough.

After, he would put on his dark blue sweatshirt with the cut-off sleeves and his baseball cap that was creased and squared the right way and go to Ford Field for practice. He would stand seven feet off third base in the sun and dust during batting practice and, with each pitch, crouch a little with his arms hanging loose, then wait for the next pitch, adjusting the squared cap, looking down at the good pocket in the Japanese glove and smoothing the ground in front of him with the toe of his spikes.

After practice and after lunch, sometime in the afternoon, he would bring some guys up on the roof and before they knew what he was doing he would be hanging from the eaves trough, four stories up. He could see their faces as he pulled himself up.

Do it or don't do it, he thought, sitting there that morning, and he did it: rolled over on his stomach and let himself down gradually, holding the edge of the trough, which was round and comfortable in his hand and didn't sag, until his arms were stiff above him, his toes pointing to the alley. Count to ten, he thought. He counted to five slowly, then began counting faster and almost started to pull himself up too quickly. But he made himself relax again and pulled himself up slowly, carefully, until his arms were over the edge and he was lying on his chest.

When he was up, away from the edge of the roof, he thought: Why tell anybody? If you can do it and know you can, what more do you want? That was a funny thing, he never did tell anybody or even hint at it. He kept it to himself. But every once in a while he would take it out and think about it.

He thought about it several times that morning while he raked the beach.

"If you're not doing anything tonight," Mr. Majestyk said, "stop in and watch some TV."

"I don't know. I might do something."

"What's her name?" Mr. Majestyk grinned, sticking a hunk of pork chop in his mouth. Chewing it, he said, "McHale's Navy is on. That son of a bitch—you ever watch it?"

"I've seen it."

Donna had set the table on the porch: pork chops, scalloped potatoes, peas, applesauce, beer, homemade bread, fruit Jell-O for dessert. Ryan could hear her in the kitchen doing the pans.

"It reminds me of when I was in the service," Mr. Majestyk said. "It isn't real, 'McHale's Navy.' I don't mean we did things like McHale's. But it reminds me. You know the Seabees?"

"I think so," Ryan said.

"C.B. Construction Battalion. We maintained this airstrip on Los Negros in the Admiralty Islands. You ever hear of it?"

"I don't think so."

"New Guinea?"

Ryan nodded. He could picture it on the map, above Australia.

"Okay, north of New Guinea maybe four hundred miles," Mr. Majestyk said. "That's the Admiralties. We'd take and make bracelets and watchbands, you know, I.D. bracelets—all out of stainless or aluminum and put in these cateyes you get from the gooks. Little round stone like half a marble, brown, black, and white, maybe some green. Then we'd sell this junk to the Navy Air Force guys and, Christ, clean up. Just junk, but the hotshots would trade you a bottle of whiskey you could get thirty-five bucks for, for a piece of junk. The First Cavalry, they secured the island before we got there. But not on horses."

"They're in Vietnam," Ryan said. "I know they don't have any horses."

"This place," Mr. Majestyk said, "They went in I think on the west side of the island, where it was all coconut trees and crap; then these Seabees would knock the goddamn coconut trees down with bulldozers to cut machine gun lanes. There was a story—these guys, the First Cavalry, were still there before they went up to the Philippines and we used to sell them all kinds of crap—they were trying to take the airstrip, dug in on one side, and these Japanese Geisha babes would come walking across the strip toward them bare naked, not a stitch on, honest to Christ, and these guys would yell, 'Throw up your hands.' But they wouldn't do it, they'd just keep on coming. So they let go wham, wham—started shooting them down, and as the babes fell these grenades started going off that the babes were holding in their *armpits*. See what they were going to do? Get in among the American guys and then just lift up their arms."

"Really naked, uh?"

"Not a stitch on."

"They probably made them do it."

"Well," Mr. Majestyk said, "You know you always think of the American guys doing brave things, but the guys on the other side they must've done some brave things too." Mr. Majestyk finished his Jell-O, scraping the rim of the dish. "Were you in the service?"

"I tried to enlist, but I got turned down. This buddy of mine went in and got into Special Forces, but they wouldn't take me. I wrecked my knee in school playing football and then I wrecked my back."

"You had an accident with it?"

"No, it was just sore for a while, my back. Then one time I got out of the shower—I was playing Class C ball then——"

"You played ball?"

"In high school and then Class C."

"Yeah? I managed a team in Legion."

"I never played Legion. I played high school and Detroit Federation. Then Class C down in Texas. I was getting out of the shower and dropped the towel. I bent over to pick it up and it was like somebody put an icepick in my back—you know, down the lower part?"

"Sure, I had that."

"I was in bed two weeks. I couldn't move. You try to roll over it's the worst pain you ever had."

"Yeah, that's the sacroiliac."

"This doctor said I had a slipped disc."

"Sure, the sacroiliac, right down at the base of the spine," Mr. Majestyk said. "I'd get it and go to this osteopathic doctor. He'd work on it and I'd feel good as new."

"It doesn't bother me much now," Ryan said, "But every once in while I know it's there."

"Well, you don't have to go in the service."

Ryan spooned his Jell-O, not looking up. "I don't know, I thought maybe I might like it."

"Well," Mr. Majestyk said, "The service is all right if you like that kind of life."

As they were finishing, one of the beer drinkers from No. 11 came in, knocking first on the screen door, and asked Mr. Majestyk if he could cash a check. Mr. Majestyk said he'd be glad to and the guy from No. 11 wrote one out for a hundred dollars.

Ryan watched Mr. Majestyk go into the living room. He watched him open the cabinet above the desk and take out a metal box. He watched him count out several bills, then close the box and turn the corner into the hall.

"You always think you've brought enough," the guy from No. 11 said, "but you always need more."

"That's right," Ryan said.

The guy from No. 11 was looking into the living room. "You got a nice place."

"If you like purple," Ryan said.

He remembered Mr. Majestyk saying his daughter from Warren had picked out everything. The place wasn't decorated like a house in the north woods at all. There was purple-looking carpeting, only lighter. Purple and

73

yellow and gray drapes. A purple-and black-striped couch with silver streaks, or threads, in it, and two matching chairs. On the table in front of the window there was a lamp made out of driftwood. There were prints on the walls of streets that were probably supposed to be in Paris, with white frames. There was a hunting dog picture, too, over the black marble fireplace. There was a white portable Sylvania TV and facing it, Mr. Majestyk's chair. It had to be his chair, a black vinyl Recline-O-Rama, because Ryan could see Mr. Majestyk sitting in it in his undershirt watching TV with a picture pillow of the Mackinac Bridge behind his head. His daughter from Warren, Michigan, may have decorated the house, but Mr. Majestyk himself must have added all the signs on the built-in cupboard doors and other places:

DANGER, MEN DRINKING

THERE'S ONLY ONE THING MONEY CAN'T BUY—POVERTY

I MISS IKE. HELL, I EVEN MISS HARRY.

And over the desk the miniature red carpet with the gold crest. OFFICIAL RED CARPET WELCOME. WE'RE MIGHTY GLAD YOU CAME!

The signs were all right, but they didn't seem to go with the furniture. That was it, the place looked like it should be in Detroit, not up here. He should have, like, maple furniture you could put your feet on and a stone fireplace with the white stuff between the stones, the mortar.

Ryan watched Mr. Majestyk come into the living room from the hall. He opened the metal box again, taking a roll of bills out of his pocket.

"I don't want to put you out," the guy from No. 11 called in.

"No trouble at all," Mr. Majestyk said.

There was a piece of vacant frontage next to Mr. Majestyk's house. It wasn't owned by Mr. Majestyk, but he told Ryan to police it up anyway and bury all the debris. It was close to the Bay Vista and looked lousy with the beer cans and what was left of beach parties. Ryan fooled around with it, picking up cans and throwing them into

74

the brush where the V.C.'s were dug in. He'd have to get the bulldozer to clear the heavy stuff, the charred logs and stones, and to dig a hole with. Come across the beach with the blade high, as a shield against the V.C. automatic weapons. Imagine doing that, cutting the machine gun lanes while the mothers were shooting at you.

He picked up a beer can, took two half steps, and threw it on a line into the brush.

"Nice arm," Mr. Majestyk said. He was at the edge of his front lawn; Ryan hadn't seen him come up.

"I used to have one. I don't know where it went."

"What'd you play?"

"Third mostly. Three summers in Class C. Then two summers I didn't play because of my back. I tried out again in June; my back felt okay and I figured I could make it."

"Yeah?"

"But just two years out of it, sitting around, made a difference."

Mr. Majestyk grinned. "You feel it already. Just wait, buddy." He looked up at the sky and said then, "It's going to rain. When it starts to blow like that."

Ryan looked up. "The sun's out."

"Not for long," Mr. Majestyk said. "You might as well go into town and get the paint; you won't be able to work outside."

"What paint?"

"Paint. What do you mean, what paint?"

"How do I know what paint you're talking about?"

"I'll tell you," Mr. Majestyk said. "How will that be?"

Dumb bastard. He was right about the rain, though. Ryan had the windshield wipers going before he was halfway to Geneva Beach. By the time he was in town and had found a place to park, the sky was overcast and the rain was coming down steadily.

There was more traffic for a weekday, more people with the same idea: in town because there was nothing to do. People, mostly kids and teen-agers, running for stores and standing in the doorways, the cars creeping along and stopping double-parked to let them out or pick them up.

It was funny how people didn't like to get wet. Ryan walked, he didn't hurry; and if he got wet, so what? What was wrong with getting wet?

He got the paint, then stopped in the drugstore for cigarettes, a bottle of Jade East, and the new issue of *True*. Coming out he saw the sky was clearing, brightening, with the sun beginning to show. He put the paint in the back of the station wagon, got in, and started the engine. A little sooner maybe, or later, he probably would have missed Billy Ruiz, but there he was coming toward the car, running hunch-shouldered and grinning. Billy Ruiz got in and slammed the door.

"Man, I thought you left!" He was touching the seat and the edge of the dashboard. "You got a car!"

"The guy I work for."

"Work—where you working?"

"A place out the Beach Road." Ryan hesitated, watching Billy Ruiz and seeing the surprise and the grin still on his face. "The Bay Vista."

"Sure, I know where that is. You work there, uh?"

"Since yesterday."

"Man, pretty soft."

"I'm not staying there, I work there."

"Yeah, with all that stuff walking around in the bathing suits, uh?" Billy Ruiz's grin stretched wider. "Don't tell me, baby."

"It beats picking cucumbers."

"Anything would beat it."

"You almost got them in?"

"A few more days," Billy Ruiz said. "They bring out these nice boys from Bay City and Saginaw as pickers yesterday? Christ, they can't pick their nose. Half of them don't show up this morning."

"More work for you."

"I got enough. Hey, you didn't hear about Frank?"

"What'd he do now?"

"He got laid off."

"Come on, you're shorthanded."

"I mean it. He's been drunk all the time, you know, with the money? He don't show up yesterday. He don't

76

come out this morning, so Bob Junior fires his ass and tells him to get out."

"What's he drinking for?"

Billy Ruiz frowned. "Because he's got money, what do you think?"

"Dumb bastard."

"Sure. Tell him that."

"Did he go home?"

"He say his truck won't make it to Texas."

"All he's got to do is get on a bus."

"You can't tell him anything, that guy."

Ryan drove Billy Ruiz to the migrant camp—to the road leading into the camp—dropped him there and headed back to Geneva thinking about Frank Pizarro and his slick hair and his sunglasses and his big mouth. Frank Pizarro was a mistake. He'd remember him with all the other mistakes he had made and promised never to make again. It was easy to make promises, but, God, it was easier to fall into things.

He turned at the Shore Road and at the last second turned left again at the first block and came up behind the IGA store. There were so many cars in the parking lot he had to drive in to get a look at the throwaway stack of boxes and cartons near the door. And when he saw it, it was a pile of boxes like any pile of boxes. It could have been the same pile that was here Saturday—except that he didn't see a red Stroh's beer case.

Driving out the Beach Road, he kept thinking about the beer case, wondering about it, until he told himself to either do something about it or forget it, but quit thinking. He couldn't trace an empty beer case that had been thrown away two days ago, so forget about it. What he couldn't forget completely was Frank Pizarro. He shouldn't have ever let him get close. He should have known Frank Pizarro the first time he ever saw him. It wasn't a good feeling to have something hanging over you. Something you shouldn't have done but did.

Or something you should have done but didn't. He remembered it as soon as he saw the girl from No. 5.

He had put Mr. Majestyk's car in the garage and was

walking up the lane behind the cabanas to his room when he saw the girl and remembered it. She was backing out of her carport, edging out, in her shiny tan Corvair. Then she was looking right at him, waiting for him to reach her.

"I wondered—I thought you were going to fix my window."

He wouldn't have remembered her if she had not been coming out of No. 5. She was dressed up: white beads, a white beaded clip in her hair, sunglasses with white rims and little pearls, made up and dressed up, sweater and purse on the seat next to her.

"The window," Ryan said. "Listen, I haven't forgotten. I got tied up."

"Do you think tomorrow?"

"First thing."

"Well not too early. I *am* on vacation." She laughed. "Anytime you say."

"Fine, then." She hesitated. "Can I give you a lift? I'm going into Geneva."

"I just got back." She didn't look bad. About third string, but not really bad dressed up.

"Well, then, thank you," Virginia Murray said and backed out a little more, slowly, before finally pulling away.

What was she thanking him for?

The back door to No. 5 and the window that was supposed to be stuck were right there. Ryan looked at the window, not closely but from a few feet away. He walked off toward his room.

Later on he went up the road to the A & W Drive-In for cheeseburgers and root beer and then played a couple of rounds of Putt-Putt golf. The redhead from No. 9 was there with her little girl, the woman in tight slacks and big white earrings and a band in her hair. She looked pretty nice, but Ryan let her go; he didn't like the idea of the little girl there. By the time he got back to the Bay Vista, it was after eight. A couple of men were on the patio smoking cigars and some kids were playing shuffleboard, but most of the people were inside now, playing cards or putting kids to bed. He thought about stopping in to see

Mr. Majestyk, but then he though, What for? So he went to bed with *True*, the Man's Magazine. He read "The Traitor Hero France Forgave," skipped "The Short Happy Life of the Kansas Flying Machine," and got partway through "Stalin's $10 Million Plot to Counterfeit U.S. Money" before he said the hell with it and picked up his sneakers and went out.

EIGHT

HE LIKED BEING ALONE. NOT ALL THE TIME,
but when he was alone, he liked it. He liked it now with the surf coming in and the wind stirring in the darkness. He could be alone on a beach anywhere. The houses back up in the trees were dark shapes that could be the huts of a village. The boats lying on the beach could be sampans used by the V.C. The word was they had brought in a load of mortars and automatic weapons, Chicom supplied by the Chinese, and he was on a one-man recon patrol up north of Chu Lai somewhere; get in and chart the V.C. ammo dumps and radio positions to the fleet sitting five miles out in the stream. It was funny people were afraid of the dark. What some guys did in the war, Underwater Demolition or the Special Forces guys, moving through the jungle at night with an M-16 and their faces black, one false step and you've got a *pungi* spike up your behind. And some people would be afraid to be out here. If you could buy the nerve to sneak up on people who were waiting to kill you, then it wasn't much to sneak up on people who were afraid of the dark. It was funny, but it was also a good thing people were afraid of it.

You got used to it, that was all. You made up your mind you were going to be good at it and not panic. It was something you developed in your mind, a coolness. No, cooler than cool. Christ, everybody thought they were cool. It was a coldness you had to develop. The pro with icewater in his veins. Like Cary Grant. Pouring champagne for the broad or up on the rooftop and the guy with the steel hook instead of a hand coming at him, he's the same Cary Grant. No sweat. That was good when he threw the guy and as the guy fell his hook scraped down the metal slant of the roof, making sparks.

Cary Grant was a good jewel thief. But it never showed what he did with the jewels after he stole them. There was an Armenian guy in Highland Park who would take TV sets, clothes, furs, things like that; but what if you brought him a $100,000 diamond necklace? "Harry, I got this $100,000 diamond necklace. What'll you give me for it?" Could you see Harry?

But no more of that. Without a car and 150 miles from a pawnshop, they could keep their TV sets and suitcases. No, no more of that anyway.

During the time he had worked with the colored guy, Leon Woody, they would look for the easy ones first: newspapers on the front steps, or houses that were dark in the early evening with the shades down, or houses where the lawns needed to be cut. They would make notes on the houses they liked. They would note down what lamps were on at what time, and if the same lamps were on two or three nights in a row—one or two downstairs and one up—they would go to the front door and ring the bell and if no one answered, they'd go in.

Leon Woody's favorite way was to go up to a house in the afternoon and ring the bell. If someone answered, he would tell the person they were looking for odd jobs—painting or wall washing or cleaning up the yard. The person, the lady, would almost always say no, and Leon Woody would ask about the people next door, if the lady knew if they were home or not. Sometimes the lady would say no, they were away for the summer or in Florida, handing it to them. Leon Woody would shake his head slowly and say, "Doggone, we is sure doin' poorly," putting on his dumb-nigger act but looking at Ryan and just barely almost smiling. If the lady did have work for them, Leon Woody would say, "Oh, thank you, ma'am. We sure do 'preciate it. But seein' it's so late, maybe we best come back in the morning." And walking away from the house, he would say to Ryan, "In the morning, she-it."

If no one answered, they would park in the drive and knock at the back door. If still no one answered, they would go in, usually through a basement window, and look for luggage first, something to put stuff in. Then they would walk out the front door carrying the suitcases full of clothes, fur coats, silver, and the TV's and radios— whatever they thought was worth taking—and throw it in the car.

They had always stayed cool during the B & E's, not showing each other anything but feeling it inside. One would never say to the other, "Come on, let's go." Or look anxious to get out. The idea was to walk through it, take your time, pick up what you wanted. Once Ryan walked into the den and Leon Woody was sitting down reading a magazine with a drink in his hand. That was about the coolest until the afternoon the guy came with the dry cleaning. Ryan went to the door: he took two suits and a topcoat from the guy, thanked him, and put the clothes in a suitcase. Thanking the guy was the touch. It was a hard one to beat. Leon Woody came close the time he answered the phone and the guy calling wanted to know who the hell this was speaking and where his wife was. Leon Woody said, "Waiting for me up in the bed, man. Where do you think?" And hung up. They gave themselves a few more minutes, just enough time, and were up in the next block when the cop car pulled in front of the house.

Once Leon Woody brought along a set of power tools he had stolen somewhere and they plugged into the porch light and drilled the lock out of the front door. Ryan said it made too much noise. Leon Woody said yeah, but it seemed more like the professional way. It was good to vary the style, he maintained, so all your B & E's didn't look alike. He was a funny guy, a tall skinny jig who had played basketball in high school and got college offers but couldn't pass the entrance exams even at the jock schools.

81

Leon Woody's problem was heroin. He was strung out most of the time Ryan knew him and it was costing him fifteen, twenty dollars a day. But he was a good guy and he would have gotten a kick out of the job Sunday, walking into the house with fifty people out in front eating hamburgers.

There were lights in the darkness, but they were pinpoints, cold little dots off somewhere in the night, as far away as stars and not part of the beach, not part of now.

There was another light, faint orange, above him. The lake frontage had climbed gradually from the low rise at the Bay Vista to a steep bluff above the beach: a brush-covered slope rising out of the sand and lined every two hundred feet or so by wooden stairways that reached up into the darkness.

Ryan stared up at the slope as he walked along, as the realization that he was wasting his time sunk in and became a fact. Finally he stopped. He should have stayed in bed. What was he supposed to do, guess which stairway led to her place? Then what, if you found it? Go up and knock on the door and act casual and say, "Hello, I just happened to be walking by." The hell with it.

Nancy watched him. Above him, up on the bluff, she had watched him pass. She had watched him stop and stand for a moment gazing up the slope; now he was coming back. Nancy walked into the orange glow of the post lamp—a girl in a dark sweater and shorts and sneakers—and out of it, a dark figure again moving down the stairs to the beach.

She waited, one hand on the railing. He was staring up at the slope and not until he was almost even with her did his gaze drop and there she was, stopping him only a few strides away.

"Well, Jack Ryan," Nancy said. "What a surprise."

Ryan walked up to her and she didn't back away or shift her position. She was at ease. She had been waiting for him, expecting him, and he could feel it.

"I was taking a walk," Ryan said.

"Uh-huh."

"You think I was looking for you?"

82

"Uh-unh, you were taking a walk."

"Just up the beach, nowhere special."

"I believe it," Nancy said. "Do you want me to walk with you?"

"I was going back."

"Why don't you relax a little?"

Walking along the beach, doing something, he felt better; though he was still aware of himself walking along next to her. They didn't talk much at first, just little probing introductory questions that Nancy asked about the migrant camp and Camacho and picking cucumbers. He answered them simply: The camp was okay. He didn't worry about Camacho. Yes, picking cucumbers was hard work. They stopped to light cigarettes and he felt her hair against his cupped hands as she leaned in and saw her face clearly for a moment in the glow of the match. She was really nice-looking. The rich girl in the movies.

"You look like somebody in the movies," Ryan said.

"Who?"

"I can't think of her name."

"What type is she?"

"Like you. Dark hair, long."

"Is she sexy?"

"Yeah, I guess so."

"What was she in?"

"I can't remember right off."

"I probably didn't see it anyway. I don't go very often. Just sometimes."

They walked along in silence and Ryan said, "Do you watch any television?"

"Hardly ever. Do you?"

"If it's something good."

"Like what?"

"A war movie, something like that. Or spy stuff."

"Wow, real-life fakey drama."

"They don't have to be true, long as they're good."

"They're boring."

"Well, what do you like, then?"

"Doing something." She looked up at him with the dark hair slanting close to her eye. "Something that makes an impression. Something that leaves a mark."

"Like what?"

"I dont know. A bullet maybe. That would be a good clean example."

"Shoot somebody?"

"Shoot something—hear it go off."

"How about dynamite?"

"Beautiful. I think dynamite would really be fun."

"But you have to put in your detonators and wire the charge and string the wire out—how about a grenade?"

"Oooo, a grenade, yes! Just pull the pin and throw it."

"Or hook it up to a trip wire," Ryan said. "As a joke."

"I think I'd rather throw it," Nancy said. "The other way you might have to wait too long."

"Okay, but where're you going to throw it?"

"I'll have to think about it," Nancy said. "I picture throwing it up on a porch or through a window. Isn't that funny?"

"A guy was telling me, during World War Two the Japs would send these Geisha girls over to our lines bare naked but with grenades under their arms; then they'd come in and the American guys would tell them to put up their hands and wham."

"Do you believe that?"

"A guy told me that was there."

"I don't believe it."

"Why not?"

"Why would they walk in? Why not just throw them?"

"Because they were *ordered* to. The Geisha girls."

"Why no clothes? I think you're friend's putting you on."

"He's not a friend. He's just a guy I know."

"I'll bet he wasn't even there," Nancy said.

"I don't care," Ryan said. "Maybe it happened, maybe it didn't. I don't care one way or the other."

Nancy was looking up the slope. She stopped, her gaze holding on the bluff, and Ryan stopped with her. "How about rocks?" she said then. "What if we used rocks and pretended they were grenades."

"And do what?"

"Throw them."

"You want to throw rocks."

"Find some, come on."

A nutty broad. God, looking for rocks. Very seriously in the dark looking for rocks. It was a dumb thing to do, but he was feeling pretty good now. "Little rocks or big ones?"

"I think a little smaller than my fist," Nancy said. "They shouldn't be too heavy."

"No," Ryan said. "You can't have them too heavy. How many you need?"

"Just a few. We'll make them count."

Very nutty broad. They took their rocks and went up the next stairway they came to, up to the lawn of a house that was totally dark, partly obscured, and shadowed by trees and shrubbery.

"They're probably at the club," Nancy said, her voice low and close to Ryan.

"You know them?"

"I don't think so. Everyone along here belongs."

"You're going to throw a rock at that house?"

"Uh-huh, right through the picture window."

"Why this house? If you don't know them——"

"Because it's there," the girl said.

"Maybe they're asleep."

"What difference does it make?"

They were crouched on their knees at the edge of the bluff. As the girl rose Ryan held her arm with the back of his hand.

"Wait a minute. What do you do after you throw it?" He had taken his sneakers out of his back pockets and was putting them on now.

"I don't know. Run, I guess. Don't you run?"

"Where? You got to know where you're going. You got to have a plan."

"We'll keep going around to the front."

"To where?"

"Don't worry about it. Just stick with me, Jackie."

Jackie. Man, he started to think, what are you doing here? But Nancy was up, running crouched across the open lawn, and he was following her, running crouched because she was. It was dumb. There was no reason to hunch your shoulders. You walked in and walked out.

Hunching your shoulders didn't make it work better. You don't *hide* hunching your shoulders.

Nancy stopped within twenty feet of the picture window, which would cost three hundred dollars to replace, and threw the rock in her left hand, throwing it like a right-handed man throwing left-handed. The rock fell short, landing in the shrubbery. "Damn!" Nancy said the one word clearly. She moved in closer, somewhat crouched, turning sideways and throwing in the same motion, and the picture window, a dull reflection in the night, exploded in a shower of glass. She was gone, somewhere around the left side of the house. Ryan raised the rock in his right hand shoulder-high; he started in set to throw as he would for a play at the plate. What the hell are you doing? he thought, and threw in a quick, short motion, not looking at the window, and heard the rock strike somewhere inside the house as he took off after the girl.

"Here!" A whisper hissed from the pines near the road.

She was out of breath, her shoulders moving as she breathed. As Ryan reached her she said, "Did you hear it?"

"Did I hear it? They heard it in Geneva."

"Loud? Wow. Imagine a real grenade."

"You know, you throw like a girl. It's funny, I didn't think you would."

"Did any lights go on?" She was looking out through the branches, calming down now.

"I don't see any. I guess you're right, they're at the club."

She looked up at him. "Let's do it where people are home."

"You think that'd be fun, uh?"

"See their reaction."

"Just stand around and watch."

"I don't know." An irritable little edge in her voice. "Let's pick the house first."

The Pointe was old and overgrown with trees, a village of comfortable homes in the north woods, large homes set back from the elm trees that lined the beach drive, smaller but expensive homes on the winding lanes among dense pines and stands of birch. There were more houses than Ryan had pictured, dim shapes now in the tree darkness, soft lamplight showing windows and screened porches beyond well-groomed lawns. Here and there in driveways Ryan picked out the metal shine of automobiles, but there were no cars moving, no headlights creeping along the drive or coming suddenly through the trees. In his mind it seemed quieter than naturally quiet after the shattering sound of the window.

They followed the row of elms, drawn toward the house lights, Nancy leading, then quickly across the road to the pines that bordered one side of a two-story brick and frame Colonial.

"You like it?" Ryan asked.

"I don't know." She studied the house for a time. "Lights but no people."

"They're in back. In the kitchen. They're having a glass of milk before they go to bed."

"Let's give them one anyway. For practice."

She didn't hesitate. She took off across the lawn on an angle that would take her within twenty feet of the house; she crossed the walk that led to the front door, stopped and turned to throw left-handed. In a natural forced-play-at-second position he threw hard sidearm and heard his window explode a half count behind Nancy's: one-two, but almost as one sound. He followed her into the trees on the other side of the yard and they worked their way back to the road, crossing quickly to the elm shadows.

"There," Ryan said. "Coming out the front door."

They watched the man standing in the porch light, coming down to the walk and looking around, then going over to the two windows. Within one of the broken windows they could make out another figure, a woman.

"She's telling him to come in the house," Ryan said. "She's saying come in, you don't know who's out there in the dark."

"Just us chickens," Nancy said. "I'd like to really hear what they're saying. We're too far."

"He's going in to call the cops now."

"You think he will?"

"What would you do?"

87

"Yes, I suppose. Hey, what if we wait for the police car and when it comes—zap-zap."

"What if we went and got a beer?"

"We have to get closer to one," Nancy said. "Come on."

She moved off again through the tree shadows with Ryan behind her, watching her legs and the ground, stopping close to her when she stopped, putting his hand on her shoulder and feeling her collarbone, frail beneath his fingers. She smelled good; not of perfume but maybe powder or soap. She smelled clean.

"There it is," Nancy said. "Perfect."

He followed her gaze across the road and the deep lawn to the new-looking, low-roofed house trimmed with grilled work and bathed in a soft gray-pink spotlight rising out of the shrubbery. Dim lights showed in every room and on the screened porch that extended along the right side of the house, facing a stand of birch trees.

"A quiet party," Nancy said. "A few friends over for a tightener after dinner."

Ryan counted five on the porch. Three women. A man appeared from inside the house, coming out with a glass in each hand.

"Fresheners," Nancy said. "Tighteners and fresheners. Sometimes drinkees or martin-eyes."

"Duck," Ryan said.

Headlights, turning onto the drive, swept the trees. Close to them, as the car hurried past, they saw the Sheriff's Patrol insignia on the door. The car's rear lights moved into the darkness and, a block from them, turned bright red.

"They'll be there ten minutes," Ryan said. "Then start prowling."

"How do they expect to find anybody in a car."

"They have to go through the motions."

"Dumb official nothing."

"What?"

"Listen, this time you go around to the back of the house and put one through the kitchen window," Nancy said.

"Yeah?"

"Don't you get it?"

"You'll be in the trees by the porch watching?"

"Very good."

"We'll only have about five minutes."

"All we'll need."

"Wait a minute," Ryan said. "I don't have any more rocks."

Nancy handed him one. "If you promise to pay me back."

She moved off. Ryan watched the two red dots of light down the street as he crossed over. There were bushes here separating the houses, and a tall hedge. He moved along close to it, along the edge of the yard all the way to the house, then across the backyard, partly lit by the kitchen and breakfast room windows, to the side of the garage. If he ever ran into Leon Woody again, if Leon Woody ever got out of Milan and he ran into him, he'd say to Leon, "Hey, man, I got a new thing." Leon Woody would say, "What's that, man?" And he'd say, "Breaking windows, man. You go around at night breaking windows." And Leon Woody would say, "Breaking windows. Uh-huh, yeah, that sounds pretty good, man." For Christ sake, Ryan thought, and threw the rock through the window before he could think about it anymore.

He stepped back to the corner of the garage, partly behind it, and watched. When the man appeared in the kitchen—the man coming in and looking around and not knowing what to expect, and now the rest of them coming behind him—Ryan left. He went into the birch trees and worked his way up along the porch side of the house. He tried to pick out the girl among the trees, the shape of her in the darkness. He came up even with the porch. The girl wasn't in the trees.

She was on the empty porch. She had a bottle in her hand and two glasses, trying to pick up something else. Finally she put the bottle under her arm. Then with the two glasses in one hand and an ice bucket in the other and the bottle under her arm she pushed open the screen door with her fanny and walked across the lawn toward Ryan at the edge of the trees. See, Leon,

89

you don't just bust the windows. You bust them and then you go in and steal a bottle of whiskey and some ice. And Leon Woody would say, "Uh-huh, sure, man, you got to have the ice."

NINE

"I LIKE CRACKED LIPS."

"From the sun," Ryan said. "Out in the sun all day."

"They're more fun. I think kissing hard and sliding around is nothing."

"Yeah, well some people think it gets you up there quicker."

"Up where?" Close to him in the sand Nancy leaned in, nuzzling in, brushing the side of his face with her mouth and gently biting his lower lip.

"I'll go your way," Ryan said.

"All the way?"

He was taking his time; he wasn't going to rush it and look like some hick, but it wasn't easy to do. He said, "Do you want another drink?" Nancy shook her head. He pushed up on one elbow and put his hand in the ice bucket. "Water," he said. "How about bourbon and cold water?"

"I thought I was taking Scotch."

"You did all right."

"Thank you."

"The walking away from the porch was good. I've got a friend would have liked that."

"Someone you worked with?"

"Cleaning carpets."

"I mean the other thing. B and E. I like B and E, the sound of it. Isn't that funny? I mean it sounds so simple, two little letters."

90

"Why don't we get some ice at your place?" They were a little way down the beach from the orange post lamp on the bluff. Sitting up, Ryan could see the point of light against the sky.

"I feel like something else," Nancy said.

"Like what?"

"Cold Ducks. But there aren't any in the house." She pushed up next to him then. "I know where there are some though. Come on."

Like that. Ryan collected the bottle and ice bucket and glasses and followed her down the beach, aware that he was following her, and hurried to catch up. She was looking out at the lake, at the deep dark of the water and the lighter dark of the sky.

"There it is," Nancy said.

"I don't see anything."

"The boat."

He saw the white shape that must be a cabin cruiser lying about fifty or sixty yards out. At the same time he realized they were opposite Nancy's house, with the orange glow of the light high on the bluff above them.

"That's Ray's, uh?"

"Somebody from the club was supposed to pick it up," Nancy said, "but they haven't." She looked at Ryan. "We won't need any of that."

"What do I do with it?"

"How about putting it down?"

"And somebody finds it in front of your house?"

"So?"

"I'll bury it."

At the foot of the bluff he dug away enough sand to cover the ice bucket and glasses and the bottle. Coming back across the beach to the water, he saw Nancy was nowhere in sight. Her clothes were in a pile.

He took off his shirt and pants, folded them, and put them on the ground next to Nancy's sweater—and shorts that were dropped there; he went into the water wearing only his shorts, making himself go right in without fooling around touching the water with his toes. It wasn't deep; he was halfway to the boat before the water was up to his waist, but God, it was cold without the sun. He had to

91

go in and get wet all the way and dove out, swimming under water to get used to it. Coming up, he swam side-stroke, reaching the stern of the boat on the starboard side, pulling himself up on the side rail and ducking under the canvas top of the afterdeck.

"Where are you?"

"In here."

He followed the sound of her voice through the open hatch, down three steps into sleeping quarters, through a short passage into the lamplight of the galley. She stood in the narrow aisle opening a bottle that looked like champagne, her wet hair straight and pressed to her face. She was wearing a sweater, a black ribbed V-neck sweater that hung to her thighs.

"I like it," Ryan said.

"My party dress." Looking right at him.

"I meant the boat," Ryan said. Very good. Don't give her anything. She was waiting for him to move in, leading him along with the sweater and the look. She was playing with him and he was standing there with his cold wet shorts sticking to him.

"There's a towel in the biffy."

He came back in drying himself, looking at the polished overhead and the brass lamp. Past the refrigerator and the stainless steel sink there was another sleeping compartment forward. It was good, the brass and the polished wood, the table hinged to the wall. Snug quarters. You didn't need champagne—or Cold Ducks. He could see the label as Nancy filled two glasses.

He sat down at the table, aware of a creaking sound and the motion of the boat pulling against its anchor. It was good, all right. You could live on a boat like this and go anywhere you wanted.

"How much does a boat like this cost?"

"About twenty-five."

"Twenty-five what?"

"Thousand." She was watching him.

"Let's go for a cruise," Ryan said. "Down to Nassau."

"I've been there," Nancy said.

"On a boat like this?"

"No, a ketch, a sailboat. There were nine with the crew. Friends of mother's."

"You'd sleep right on it?"

"Most of the time."

"That'd be something," Ryan said.

"Uh-huh, sitting around all day while everybody got stoned. By five o'clock they'd be freaked out of their minds."

"You were with your mother and dad?"

"I was between dads. My mother would say, 'Darling, why don't you go below and take a rest?' Or, 'Why don't you go swimming or look for interesting shells.' Or slash your wrists—that's what she wanted to say. Everything was *interesting* at that time. 'Why don't you go talk to that interesting-looking boy. He's about your age, dear.'"

"How old were you?"

"Fourteen."

"Do you get along with her now?"

"I don't see her now."

"Does she know what you're doing—I mean, where you are?"

"Did you tell your mother you stole things?"

"I don't do that anymore," Ryan said.

"When you were B and E-ing, or whatever you call it? Did you tell her?"

"No."

"I told old mom I was shacked up with Ray Ritchie," Nancy said. "But she won't think about it. She likes everything *nice*." Nancy stretched the word out sweetly.

"Well, what do you expect?"

"I don't expect anything. She's not real. I mean on the surface she's not." Nancy felt the cigarette package and squeezed it in her fist. "Damn it, we're out."

"What do you mean she's not real?"

Nancy was thoughtful, curled on the bench across from him in the oversized sweater. "She pretends to be the perfect lady. She *is* Perfect Lady on the outside, leading a perfectly normal perfect life. But the real person is inside the perfect lady looking out and she's as screwed up as anybody, with three screwed-up marriages to prove it."

Ryan said, "She's inside this person, uh?"

"She won't admit she's in there, but she is. You can see her looking out." Nancy smiled. "That's fun, to get her to look out. She does that a lot, and sometimes she'll even stick her head out a little. But I've never been able to get her out all the way."

"I don't get it," Ryan said.

"It doesn't matter. I wish we had cigarettes," she said then. She sipped her Cold Duck and filled their glasses again. "You like?"

"It's all right."

"But you'd rather have a shot and a beer."

"One or the other."

"Good old Bob Junior is strictly beer. Ray is martinis."

Ryan hunched forward, resting his arms on the table edge. "Can I ask you a question?"

"What am I doing here," Nancy said.

"Something like that."

"Just letting it happen, I guess," Nancy said. "Looking for the bounce, like everybody else."

"Why Ray Ritchie—a guy twenty years older than you are?"

"Twenty-five, Charlie."

"All right, but why?"

"Why do you steal?"

"I told you, I don't anymore."

"Did you ever steal money?"

Ryan hesitated. "Sometimes, if there was some laying around."

"What was the most you ever got?"

"Seventy-eight bucks."

Nancy was turning the stem of her glass between her fingers slowly. "What if you came across fifty thousand laying around?" She looked up at Ryan. "Between fifty and fifty-five thousand. Would you have the nerve to take it?"

Ryan sat relaxed, keeping his eyes on her eyes, aware of the faint creaking sound again and, for what it was worth, waiting for her to make something out of the silence and the way he was looking at her. He didn't smile or make a remark or try to be funny; he didn't have to ask her if she was serious. He knew as soon as she said it that this is what it was all about: why she was here and why he was here.

Nancy said, "If you'd rather not talk about it——"

"Whose fifty thousand, Ray's?"

"Uh-huh."

"Where?"

"In his hunting lodge."

"He keeps fifty thousand in his hunting lodge. Sitting there."

"He does the night before he pays the migrants." Nancy watched him. "Multiply three hundred and fifty workers by a hundred and fifty dollars each. Isn't that the average?"

"About."

"It comes to fifty-two thousand, five hundred. Not checks, money. In pay envelopes. Three hundred and fifty envelopes in two cardboard boxes."

"How do you know?"

"From last year, and when they were paid this year after planting, or whatever they did."

"Ray brings the money? How does it get here?"

"I'm not sure," Nancy said. "Last year we were at the lodge, a police car drove up and Bob Junior got out with the boxes and put them in Ray's office, in the den."

"The money's already in the pay envelopes?"

"Uh-huh. Then the next day Bob Junior sits at a card table and they line up and he pays them."

"How do you know they always bring it the day before?"

"Bob Junior told me."

"You asked him?"

"Making conversation. He said it's the way they always do it."

"And they leave the money there, forget about it all night."

"Not exactly." Nancy paused. "Bob Junior said he stays with it. I don't know if in the same room but in the lodge."

"Well, if he's sitting on the boxes, how're we supposed to get them?"

Nancy shrugged. "I don't know. Maybe you wait till he goes to the bathroom."

"There'd have to be a way to get in," Ryan said. "If you have only a minute, you can't fool around breaking something to get in."

"What if we went in the day before and arranged it?"

Ryan finished the Cold Duck in his glass. "You sure there aren't any cigarettes?"

"I looked before."

"How long have you been thinking about this?"

"It didn't come to me until after I saw you Sunday."

"Why me?"

"Don't be modest. Because it's your bag."

"Fifty thousand isn't a TV set."

"It's lighter," Nancy said. "Think of it that way."

"I mean, why think about it at all? You've got about everything you want."

"And things I don't want." Nancy leaned in, letting her hair fall close to her face. "Let's not go into all the whys, all right?"

Ryan put his mind back on the fifty thousand. "Are you talking about splitting?"

"Of course. I'm not greedy."

"What if I take the whole thing?"

"Because you know I know and you wouldn't sleep at night until you were arrested."

"After we get it, then what? How do we get away?"

"We don't," Nancy said. "We hide the money."

"Where?"

"In the beach house."

"Come on."

"Really. It's the best place; right under Ray's nose. You stay in Geneva Beach until Ray closes the place for the summer, then break in and get it. I'll stay with him for about two weeks after we're back in Detroit, then we'll have a fight and I'll leave him."

"We meet in Detroit," Ryan said. "Then what?"

Nancy smiled, hunching her shoulders like a little girl. "I don't know. What do you want to do?"

"I think I'd want to rest awhile."

"Or take a cruise. The kind I was telling you about?"

"I could get my own boat."

"And a car and new clothes. Anything you want."

Ryan nodded, thinking about it. "Just about anything." He looked at her. "What about you? What do you want?"

Nancy took a sip of Cold Duck. "Do you really want to know?"

"Sure, tell me."

"I might go out to Hollywood. I think twenty-five thousand would be just enough of a stake."

"You mean it?"

"Why not? Hook myself a producer. A nice *rich* producer."

"Just like that."

"I think I could fake most of them out of their socks in about four minutes."

"You mean out of their jocks."

She shrugged. "I bet I could."

"Do you know how to act?"

"Fake that too," Nancy said. "That's what acting is, isn't it?"

"You're not planning on us staying together, then."

Nancy shrugged again. "I don't know. Right now I don't need a lover, Jackie, I need a breaking and entering man."

Jackie again. He didn't say anything.

"I want the money," Nancy said. "If I have to justify wanting it, then it's because I think Ray owes it to me. You can do it for whatever reason you like. I'm not your conscience."

"All right, you want me to think about it?"

"If you can't say yes or no right now."

"You've been thinking about it awhile, I haven't."

"It's fairly simple," Nancy said. "You either want it or you don't."

"I have to look at the lodge first," Ryan said. "Then I'll let you know."

"Tomorrow's Wednesday. If they're bringing the money Friday, you won't have much time."

"Maybe I can borrow this guy's car I work for. Go over there sometime tomorrow. Tell him I got to get something in town."

"Creepy Ray," Nancy said. "He took my keys or you could use mine."

Ryan nodded. "I heard you had a car." He tried to picture her running the two guys off the road and he wanted to ask her about it, but he said, "What if I could start your car?"

"Without a key?"

"If you can get me some wire, it's done."

It was a friend of Ryan's, Bud Long, who had taught him how to jump wires: how to short out the starter and run a wire from the battery to the coil, making sure to hook it on the right side of the coil so it wouldn't burn out the points. Bud Long worked for a loan company in Detroit, on Livernois, up among the miles of used car lots, and most of the paper the company carried was for car loans. When a customer got behind in his payments and wouldn't acknowledge receiving the payment notices, Bud Long would go out at night and repossess the car with a jump wire. Sometimes Ryan and one or two others would go with him for something to do and Bud Long would let them jump the car. Usually they drove off and that was it. But a couple of times, when somebody saw them, they had to leave the car fast with the hood up and the wire hanging, cutting between houses to Bud Long's car parked on the next street. Once they took a 16-gauge shotgun blast in the rear quarter panel, but they got away. (Bud Long said the son of a bitch probably owed money on the shotgun too.)

That was all right, jumping cars with Bud Long; it was legal, or at least it seemed legal, and Bud knew what he was doing. But then a couple of the other guys started jumping cars when they wanted to go somewhere and didn't have a ride and it was dumb to get involved in that. Ryan rode with them a few times when they came by for him. They'd drive the car downtown or wherever they were going and leave it. But one time—two thirty in the morning on East Jefferson near the Uniroyal plant— the dumb son of a bitch he was with, Billy Morrison, threw an empty beer bottle out the window with a cop car a half block behind them. They were pulled over, checked, and taken to the station on Beaubien and charged with car theft. Ryan called the older of his two sisters, Marion, whose husband was a lawyer, and told him what happened, and his brother-in-law, Carl, a sweetheart, told him to stay in jail, maybe it would teach him a goddamn lesson. He was arraigned on the warrant the next day, pleading not guilty; his bond was set at $500. But because he couldn't afford the bond without his brother-in-law's help, he spent eight days in the Wayne County Jail. At the Examination, Carl talked to Billy Morrison's lawyer, the two of them standing, nodding at each other with the briefcases under their arms, and before he knew it, he and Billy Morrison had copped a plea of guilty to the charge of Unlawfully Driving Away an Automobile, UDAA, and were sent to Morning Sessions Court. Because it was their first offense, they were both placed on a year's probation and his brother-in-law took him out to lunch so they could "have a little talk."

The next day—and this, Ryan figured, must be the world's record for poor timing—he was back in Morning Sessions sitting on the bench in the fenced-off section with the stew bums and colored hookers waiting to go before the same judge. Not Billy Morrison and Jack Ryan this time. Just Jack Ryan.

It was poor timing and it was also dirty rotten luck of the worst kind because it should never have happened.

He had gone to lunch with Carl for the little talk; he had gone to a movie and then home. He had to go home sometime, so he went home.

They were still living in the apartment in Highland Park: he and his mother and, for the past seven months, his other sister, Peggy, and her husband, Frank, who worked at a bakery on the night shift. Ryan was sleeping on the studio couch in the dining room again. The three of them were there when he got home. His mother told him how worried she had been and how Carl had told her not to visit him in jail or go to the court hearing. He remembered they had already eaten. (They ate at 5:30 because Frank had to leave for work by quarter to seven and he liked to sit and watch TV and let his dinner digest.) But they hadn't saved anything because they didn't know Jack was coming home. He remembered his mother looking in her purse, then asking Frank didn't she loan him five dollars last week?—asking him twice because he was watching TV, sitting in his T-shirt with his stringy neck and his dark hair combed in a high roll, his sister Peggy sitting next to Frank, sitting straight with bobby pins in her mouth, putting her hair up, and Frank finally saying he had already paid her back. Ryan said he had money and he remembered his mother saying don't go to Major's, go down to Safeway, the hamburger was three pounds for a dollar ten this week. He remembered her saying that pork roasts were on sale, too, and if he saw a nice one and had enough extra money, they could have it for Sunday; Frank was bringing home a pie. He remembered her saying she wished there was an A&P in the neighborhood and he remembered, going out the door, his sister saying yes, A&P was all right, but you didn't get any stamps there.

He didn't go to Safeway. He went to a bar on Woodward up near Seven Mile and drank beer. Maybe they were still talking about the A&P. The way it was before and the way he would always remember it, his father would be in the dining room playing solitaire and his mother would be in the living room with the radio on, the thin, slick-haired man and the lady beginning to get fat. They hardly ever spoke to each other. His mother would bring up the worn carpeting or that she had seen a nice-looking graduation dress for Peggy and his dad would say, "Uh-huh, all right. Fine." With the cigarette smoke curling up past his eyes, squinting down at the cards. Ryan had wondered if they ever made love. The slick-haired man with his hair combed and his teeth brushed and the beginning-to-get-fat lady lying there wondering if they should trade the Bendix washer in or try to get another year out of it. The man would be smoking a cigarette after and the lady would finally say, "You know, we've had that Bendix nine years." Ryan couldn't picture them first meeting or dating or the way they were before he was born. But something must have happened. Something, and he would bet anything it was because of money. Counting pennies to buy hamburger. Maybe that tightens you up and once it does, you stay tightened. His dad was different sometimes when they were alone. He would seem to know about things. He would say ask me a capital and Ryan would ask it and his dad would know it. Even Central America. He would know all about places like Guadalcanal and Tarawa and tell about times men had lost their lives because the brass had screwed up, miscalculated, though he had not been in the war himself. He would tell what was wrong with the DSR, how they didn't have enough buses and how the jigs were getting all the good runs because the big shots were afraid of the racial situation. (Later, when Ryan was working with Leon Woody, he wondered what his dad would have thought of it. He wondered if he would have started breaking into houses if his dad hadn't died. And then he would think: Why? What's that got to do with the price of anything? And he would think about something else.)

When Billy Morrison came into the bar, he felt like decking the son of a bitch, but Billy was grinning and looked really glad to see him, so they drank beer and celebrated the neat way they'd beat the larceny charge. About 11:30 Billy Morrison said how about a little action? Ryan thought he meant pick up some broads somewhere, but Billy said, man, they didn't have time for that; it had to be a sure thing. Not if it costs money, Ryan said. Billy said come on, it's a new kick, and Ryan went with him to a gas station over on John R.

A gas station. This was about the craziest thing he'd ever heard of. Billy Morrison said, man, like getting your oil changed. The station attendant dialed a number. They waited about twenty minutes smoking cigarettes before a Pontiac station wagon pulled in with two guys in front, young guys, and a girl in back about sixteen with long, tangled brown hair and a tight skirt way up on her thighs. After you, Billy Morrison said, and Ryan got in the back seat with the girl. She was pretty, but she had on too much perfume and he didn't like her hair; he didn't like the two guys; he didn't like anything about it, sitting in the dark with the three of them as they drove south on John R toward Six Mile. The guy next to the driver asked him if he wanted a beer. Well. Why not? He took the warm beer from the guy and the guy said that would be a buck. Ryan said nothing; he paid him. He asked the girl if she wanted some and she said no. That was all she said in the car. The one word. The two in front talked sometimes but mostly to each other and Ryan couldn't hear what they were saying. He remembered how quiet it was in the car. Then the sound of his own voice asking where they were going. The guy next to the driver said over by a school yard. Sometimes they went to a park or over to a lumber yard, but tonight it was the school yard. There was a blanket in the back, the guy said. Ryan sipped the warm beer. After a minute, breaking the silence again, he asked how much it would be for all this great service and everything and the guy next to the driver, without turning around, said ten bucks.

Ryan said they had better drive him back, he wasn't buying anything today after all. Ahead of them he could see the stoplight at Six Mile Road. They were approaching it, but the car slowed down and turned left into an alley before they reached the corner. The car stopped; the headlights beamed down past trash cans and incinerators and the shadowed back walls of stores. The headlights went off and the guy next to the driver, thin-faced with long hair, about Ryan's age, turned with his arm on the backrest. He said it would cost ten bucks. He said whether they took Ryan to the school or back to the gas station or anywhere, it would cost ten bucks. Ryan said no, he had changed his mind. The guy looking at him said, man, nothing was free. Everything cost ten bucks. Ryan said okáy, I'll make you a deal. You don't have to drive me back. I'll get out here.

The inside light went on as the driver opened his door. Ryan remembered seeing the girl, her hair lighter than he thought it would be; he remembered feeling the beer running up his sleeve, colder than it had tasted, as he raised the bottle by the neck and saw the guy next to the driver drop behind the backrest. Ryan was out, slamming the door, moving along the car to the rear, then sliding in the gravel and changing his direction. As the driver came past the front end Ryan went into him, chopping the bottle

102

against the side of his head backhanded so that the guy fell against the hood.

The bottle didn't break. In the movies the bottle breaks, but this one didn't. He held onto it and ran, all the way down the alley and right, past the brick side of a store to Six Mile, across the street and east along the sidewalk, not aware that he was still holding the bottle. He was in the next block when he felt the car moving along next to him. He didn't want to look at the car, he wanted it to pass and he wanted to keep walking.

But the car didn't pass and he did a dumb thing. He looked at the car because he had to, a car that as soon as he looked at it was a black-with-yellow-lettering police car. And he ran. He didn't think, he ran. Later, thinking about it, he realized what a dumb thing he did and made a resolution it would never happen again; but later was too late. He ran to the corner and around it; he ran down the length of a cyclone fence, down to the end of it and up over the fence. He hid in the darkness and silence against the wall of the lumber company, in the aisle between ten-foot stacks of two-by-fours, and he was standing there with the beer bottle in his hand when they put the flashlight on him. He held the beer bottle half raised at his side, the light in his eyes, and finally he let go of it.

The judge at Morning Sessions, a nice calm-looking guy with his hair starting to get gray at the sides, gave him sixty days in the Detroit House of Correction.

He had had enough bad luck. It was time to have some good luck. There had to be a beginning to the good luck if he was going to have any, and maybe this was the beginning. It was good to have a car again. It was good driving along at night with the radio on. It was good rolling into the Bay Vista and angle-parking in front of the office. If this was the beginning of the good luck, he would have to watch and be ready and, finally, at one point, if it still looked good, he would have to say yes and step into it and do it, go all the way.

Why would it be any harder than going into a house for TV sets and fur coats? Or any harder than walking into his own room.

From the bed, sitting across it against the wall and his cracked curl-toed boots sticking out over the side, Frank Pizarro said, "Hey, Jack, how you doing?"

"Get off the bed."

"What's the matter with you?" Pizarro pushed himself to the edge and sat with his legs hanging, not touching the floor.

"How'd you know I was here?"

"Billy tole me. What's the matter with you?"

"I mean this room."

"A guy outside, when I came. I ask him."

"He tell you to walk in, make yourself at home?"

"No, I wait out there awhile, then I think maybe you sleeping and don't hear me, so I try the door and it's open. Listen, I got fired from my job."

"I heard."

"From Billy. But he didn't tell you about the bus."

"Frank, I'll see you, okay?"

"Listen, Camacho wants me to drive the bus back for the money I owe him. Drive him in it and leave my truck because the goddamn thing's busted anyway."

Ryan hesitated. "That's fine with me."

"Sure, but how do the rest of them get home? See?"

"In the bus."

"No. Camacho say, 'I don't have to take them home.' I say, 'But they already pay you to take them.' He say, 'That was when I was crew leader. But I'm not crew leader no more, so I don't have to take them.' He say then, 'But if they want to pay my bus company five hunnert dollar and give me money for the airplane, then I leave the bus here.'"

"Come on. They believe that?"

"What are they going to do? They tell him they don't like it, Camacho leave them here."

"What do you care? You've got a ride."

"What do I care? They all my friends."

"Come on, Frank."

"I mean it. I work with them seven years."

"All right, so why come to me?"

"Man, we been friends, right? Billy say, 'Why don't we

borrow the money from Jack?' Pizarro's flat, open face stared up at Ryan.

"Five hundred dollars."

"Billy say you got it. He say if you spent it, you can get some more easy."

"Where is Billy?"

"He don't want to come. You know, to ask you."

"It doesn't bother you any."

"Listen, I don't ask you for the money. Billy say that. I want to borrow it from you and we pay you back."

"You think I have five hundred?"

"You don't, you can get it. Easy."

"If I loaned you what I have, you'd pay it back, uh?"

"You know that. Sure."

"When?"

"Next year when we come up."

"It's been nice knowing you, Frank."

"Man, we got these families. How they going to get home?"

"Come on—I've got *this* family."

"You don't care what happens to all those people?"

"Hey, Frank, I'll see you."

"Okay, buddy," Pizarro said. He came off the bed slowly. "Screw you too."

Pizarro moved past him and opened the door; narrow shoulders and drooping pants seat, checkered pants that were worn and dirty, shapeless, with slash continental pockets and a snappy snap-around elastic waist.

"Wait a minute," Ryan said. "You got your truck?"

"I tole you, it's busted."

"You going to walk?"

"No, I'm going to rent a goddamn Hertz car."

Ryan hesitated, watching Pizarro holding the door open, but only a moment. He said, "See you, Frank."

Pizarro noticed the Mustang in front of the office. He looked at the car as he walked past it and something about it was familiar. There were a lot of dark green Mustangs, but there was something else about a Mustang that stuck in his mind. He walked down to the first side road beyond the Bay Vista and got his panel truck out of the trees and headed for Geneva Beach as fast as the rusted-out panel would move. But by the time he got there, the bars and liquor stores were closed and the town was locked up for the night. Goddamn Ryan.

Waiting for Ryan and not finding anything to drink in Ryan's place, he had thought of getting a bottle of something, tequila or gin. Or a bottle of red. If he bought wine, he'd have a few bucks left over. He had four dollars and sixty cents of the hundred Ryan had given him as his cut. Sure he had waited in the truck. But, goddamn, it was his truck; he was the one to drive it. At the time he should have pulled off the road and laid it on him. "Hey, man, where's my cut? No chickenshit hunnert dollars, *my cut*." Lay it on him and let him know. Ryan had been lucky with Camacho; but that didn't mean he was always lucky.

He had never liked Ryan. Ever since San Antonio, at the gas station: Ryan standing there with his bag looking for a ride, standing there with his hands on his hips looking them over as they pulled in—the bus, the panel truck, and two cars, all migrants; then talking to Camacho for a while and getting in the bus. Ever since then. Ever since, on the trip up, Ryan started going into the stores where they had trouble being served to get the pop and stuff to make sandwiches. Ever since in the town in Oklahoma talking the gas station man into letting them use his stinking broken-down washroom, thinking he was a big shot because he did it. Ever since he started talking to Marlene Desea and before they were out of Missouri had got her to leave the panel truck and ride in the bus with him. Somebody else, one of the other girls, had said, "Frank, I would love to ride with you." But he had told her nothing doing, nobody was riding with him now.

Camacho was right—what he said after they had reached the cucumber fields—that Ryan only wanted a ride. He got what he wanted and there was nothing to keep him—not Marlene Desea, not anything. He used the truck. He used Billy Ruiz. He used everybody and once he got what he wanted, he left. Sure, that's the kind of guy.

Beyond Geneva Beach, on the highway south, he turned off on the dirt road that pointed through the fields to the migrant camp.

Goddamn cucumbers. He was through with the cucumbers. He could pick ten times more than the goddamn kids they sent up from Saginaw and Bay City, but if they wanted the kids instead of him, that was up to them. He had drunk a little too much since Saturday, a hundred dollars worth almost, but buying the others a lot of it too. It was gone, the hundred, and he owed Camacho four hundred fifty dollars and he didn't have a job and San Antonio was sixteen hundred and seventy miles away.

But Ryan wasn't gone. Man, he had Ryan. All he had to do was think of a way to tell him, a good way to tell him without getting his jaw broken. Like:

"Hey, Jack. You know that beer case with the wallets you tole us to throw away? We don't throw it away, man. I got it hid somewhere."

Then Ryan would say something and he would say to Ryan, "How much you give me for that beer case, buddy? So somebody don't find it with your name on it."

That would be the difficult part, to tell Ryan so he would see clearly that he had no choice but to buy the case of wallets. "Look, you swing at me, you never see the beer case, you understand?"

The son of a bitch, you didn't know what he might do. Tell him quick, "Something happen to me a friend of mine take the beer case to the police. How you like that, buddy?"

Then tell him how much. Five hundred dollars for the case. No, six hundred dollars. He don't have it, he has to work for it then, go in some places.

He had planned to tell Ryan tonight. Begin with the phony story about the bus and see if he could get some money that way, the easy way. Then tell him about the beer case. But when Ryan came in and was standing there, he couldn't do it.

Maybe get some paper and write it to him. Buy the paper and get a pencil somewhere. Write it clearly and some night put it under his door. But he would have to see Ryan sooner or later, or else how would he get the money from him? Goddamn, why did it have to be so hard to do?

For a reason Frank Pizarro would never be sure of— other than he might have seen the car with the girl in it going past the camp, going past this shed where he was now stopping—he remembered the dark green Mustang and remembered at once who owned it. Mr. Ritchie's girl friend. Sure, the same green Mustang with the dents in the front end, the same dents in the same car in front of Jack Ryan's place.

Pizarro turned off the engine and the headlights, but he didn't get out right away. He kept thinking about the green Mustang because he knew goddamn well Jack Ryan had something to do with it.

TEN

"IT'S A GOOD DEAL," MR. MAJESTYK SAID. "Thirty bucks a week she comes in every day but Sunday. Sunday I like to cook a steak outside on the grille, nice sirloin, this guy at the IGA cuts it about two and a half inches thick."

Mr. Majestyk sliced off a piece of kielbasa and dipped it in chili sauce. He pushed the fork into his sauerkraut and heaped it over the sausage with his knife. Chewing, he took a piece of bread and buttered the whole slice. Still chewing, he said, "She bakes it herself. At home, bakes two, three times a week and brings it in fresh. I mean fresh."

"It's all right," Ryan said.

"She keeps the place clean. Vacuums twice a week."

Ryan was eating fast. He had missed breakfast again and he was hungry. The idea had been to get up early and drive over to Ritchie's hunting lodge and look it over, before anybody was around. But he'd overslept and missed breakfast. He'd have to drive out there after work, but he was too hungry to think about that now. "She can cook," Ryan said.

"I wouldn't let her if she couldn't," Mr. Majestyk said.

"You got something going with her?"

"With Donna?" Mr. Majestyk glanced toward the doorway into the living room. "Christ, what do you think, I'm hard up or something?"

"She's old, but she's not too bad-looking," Ryan said. "I mean, better than nothing."

"You're young, you got it on the brain."

"Well, it's natural, isn't it?"

"Natural doesn't mean you got to think about it all the time."

"Is that right? What do you think about?"

"I got plenty of things," Mr. Majestyk said. "For example, should I stay up here year-round? I mean, what's in Detroit? I might as well live here. I mentioned keeping the place open for hunting season?"

"You said something about it."

"Well, I got another idea. A hunting lodge."

"Like Ritchie's?"

"Naw, that's a farmhouse he fixed up. You know what an A-frame is?"

"I'm not sure."

"Like a Swiss-looking place—a steep roof almost comes down to the ground? For people who ski. They're building them all over up north. Prefab."

"I've seen pictures."

"Take two of them," Mr. Majestyk said. "Big ones, each sleeps about ten with the loft upstairs, and join them together with a central heating system."

"You already got the cabins," Ryan said.

"I'd have to put in new heating units. It gets twenty below, them little units in there would quit. No, I don't mean here. There's some property I know a guy wants to sell—off by itself, woods, a lake. You know the road there it goes through the migrant camp and up past Ritchie's lodge?"

"Yeah?"

"Go past it about a half a mile, you see a sign, ROG-ERS, turn left and follow the road up the hill through the woods."

"Out away from everything."

"Right. Build the A-frames there, get twenty hunters, twenty-five bucks a day each—three full meals, all the mix and ice and everything included for twenty-five bucks a day."

"That'd be all right."

"In the heart of deer country. But you see with the lake you got the bird hunters too. These guys—Christ, I know a dozen guys I could call, they wouldn't hesitate. And they all got friends who hunt."

"Why don't you do it?"

Mr. Majestyk stared at Ryan, then shrugged. "Maybe. I don't know."

"You'd make five hundred bucks a day."

"Gross. Yeah, but I'd need a guy, maybe a couple of guys who could cook, you know, and knew how to handle guns."

"What's the problem?"

"No problem, just finding the right guys. You know anything about guns?"

"I used to sell them," Ryan said, "Hunting rifles, shotguns, at this sporting goods store."

"I thought you were a cook?"

"Yeah, I did that too. Fry chef."

"Are you a good cook?"

"Sure. It was mostly these chefburgers, but lunch-time you'd have everything going—filets, fried eggs, pancakes, club sandwiches. The waitresses would call the orders and you had to keep it all going."

"For a young guy," Mr. Majestyk said, "I guess you've done a few things."

"A few." He told Mr. Majestyk about working at The Chef and the sporting goods store and at Sears but didn't mention the carpet cleaning job because that was where he had met Leon Woody.

A friend of Ryan's had the job first. The friend

wanted to quit and go to electronics school, but he didn't want to let his boss down, he said, so he told Ryan about it. Good pay, not too hard, these big, beautiful homes you work in, and the woman, these rich babes, honest to God you wouldn't believe it what some of them wear around the house, showing you the goodies, boy, some of them just asking for it. Ryan said, yeah? And his friend said, you know, bending over to do something and no bra on? Or these babes that let their housecoats come undone?

Ryan never did see anything like that. He seldom saw anyone at all except when they arrived and when they left. He realized after a few weeks that the guy had been pulling his chain about the women, but that was all right. He liked the job. What he liked about it especially was being in a strange house and seeing personal things that belonged to people he didn't know. It wasn't the same as being in a friend's house. It gave him a funny feeling, especially when he was alone in a room, in the silence after he had turned off the machine, or alone going up the stairs to do a bedroom. It was a feeling as if something was going to happen.

Until this time Ryan hadn't stolen anything since grade school when they used to steal combs and candy bars from the dime store. The only big things he had ever stolen and ever thought about were a baseball glove, hat, spikes, and a green jersey with yellow sleeves from Sears. It wasn't too hard. Everybody on the 8th-grade team did it, making about four trips each at different times with raincoats or shopping bags, twelve guys and not one was caught, though two guys got the wrong color jerseys and when they went back, they were out of the green and yellow.

It was a time Ryan was working in a room alone that he thought of coming back to the house later. The woman happened to mention they were leaving for Florida the next day. Ryan thought about it while he worked, trying to imagine the feeling of being alone in the house at night. He began to wonder then if he had enough nerve to go into a house while the people were sleeping, or not knowing if they were asleep or awake

111

or what. God, you'd have to be good to do that. But if you were sure of the layout of the house, if you were sure there wasn't a dog, and if you had a good way to get in, it could be done.

He was working with Leon Woody when he thought of the way to do it. They would move the furniture out to the middle of the floor and shampoo the carpeting around the walls first, then move the furniture back and put aluminum foil pads under the legs. Ryan positioned an end table, reached into the draperies, and unlocked a side window. He pulled his hand out and saw Leon Woody watching him.

Leon Woody shook his head, grinning. Ryan said, "What's the matter with you?"

Leon Woody said, "Nothing," still grinning.

He didn't bring it up until they were in the truck. He said, "Man, why would you want to get the company in trouble? You want to go in, pick a house we haven't been to."

Ryan told him he was crazy or didn't know what he was talking about. Something like that.

"You think I don't know?" Leon Woody said. "I've been watching you looking around. Let me tell you something. You go in where they're home and sometime some hero is going to blast your ass, man. You go in when they're *not* home, when you *know* it and have it in writing they're not home."

"You've done it?"

"Do it, man. I do it."

"I've only done it once."

"And about to do it again."

"I wasn't going to take anything."

Leon Woody looked at him. "Then, why do you want to go in?"

"I don't know." It sounded dumb. "Just to see if I can, I guess." It still sounded dumb.

"Like, man, a game?"

"Yeah, sort of."

"You know what you get if you lose the game?"

"That's part of it. The risk. There's got to be a risk."

"What's the other part?"

"Seeing if you can do it, I guess."

"No baby, that's not the other part. The other part is a white Mercury convertible and fifteen suits and twelve pairs of shoes and I don't know how many chicks I can call anytime of the night. *Anytime.*"

"If you want money," Ryan said, "that's something else."

"Man, it's the whole something else. You going to tell me you don't want it?"

"Sure, everybody wants enough to live on. I mean to live well."

"Do you live well?"

"I get along."

"Do you live well?"

"Not that you'd call, you know, comfortably."

"Well, man," Leon Woody said, "let's make you comfortable."

It was hard, when he thought about it, not to think of it as a game. A kick. He was breaking the law and knew he was breaking it, but he never thought of it that way. It was funny, he just didn't. It was wrong to break into somebody's house, okay, but he wasn't taking anything they really *needed*. A TV set, a mink jacket, a couple of watches, all insured; maybe they'd get two-fifty, three hundred for the load. The insurance company pays off and the guy buys another TV set, another fur for his wife, and a couple of watches, everything at a discount because he's a big shot and has all kinds of *ins*. The guy probably got the money to buy the stuff in the first place by screwing somebody in business. It was all right in business, but it wasn't all right going through a basement window. Why not?

Maybe that didn't follow. Maybe you couldn't justify going through the window, but how many things in your life did you bother to justify? If you got caught, you got caught. No excuses. No trying to skinny out. Right? That was the only way to think about it. Though the best way was not to think about it at all. Just do it and don't make a big thing out of it.

In spite of Leon Woody, he still had to go into a

place not knowing whether the people were home or not, and finally he did it. The first time he stayed downstairs, felt his way around, and left in a couple of minutes, not taking anything. The next time he went up to the second floor, keeping to the side of the steps, putting his weight gradually on each step, until he was in the upstairs hall. He walked into a bedroom where a man and a woman were sleeping and took seventy-eight dollars out of a billfold on the dresser. He was going to tell Leon Woody about it, but at the last second, ready to tell him, he decided to keep it to himself. Leon Woody might think he was nuts.

Finally, though, he didn't have to worry about Leon Woody or what he thought. Twice Leon Woody was picked up on suspicion. Somehow the police got onto him. They went into his place with warrants and wanted to know how he could afford the car and all the expensive clothes. Leon Woody told them gambling—horses, man. The third time Ryan and Leon were both picked up. They had gone into a house and, on the way home, stopped for a couple of beers. They weren't in the bar a half hour, but when they came out, two plainclothesmen were waiting at Leon's car with a warrant. Ryan was arraigned with Leon on a charge of breaking and entering and was given a suspended sentence. Leon drew six months for possession of stolen property. He also lost his job with the carpet cleaner. After his release he was arrested again, this time for possession of narcotics, and was sent to the Federal Correction Institution at Milan. Ryan wrote to him for a while, but Leon Woody hardly ever answered. He probably had something going at Milan and was too busy.

In eight months of part-time breaking and entering Ryan made about four thousand dollars. He didn't buy expensive clothes or move out of the apartment because he knew his mother would suspect something and ask questions. Though one time he brought home a stolen TV set when the one at home had blown a picture tube, and no one—not his mother or his sister

114

or Frank, his brother-in-law—asked him where he got it.

In June, Ryan took a Greyhound to Texas for another try at Class C ball.

"It's being inside all the time that gets you," Mr. Majestyk said. "That's why I sold the tavern. You got to get out and do what you want to do and feel you own yourself. You know what I mean?"

"When I quit the job at Sears," Ryan said, "that's the way I felt."

"Sure, I know what you mean. What about the baseball?"

"I told you, I got this bad back."

"I mean when did you play Class C?"

"It was just three summers, I thought I told you," Ryan said. "I'd work at these jobs the rest of the year. Then two summers I didn't play because of my back. Then it felt okay and I tried out again this June, figuring I could make it."

"Yeah?" Mr. Majestyk was interested.

"But my back—I don't know, it gave me a hitch in my swing. A guy would curve me and I'd get all out of shape. So I come home, figure forget it."

"You drove up with the migrants, uh?"

"That's right. This crew leader offered me a job, so I figured why not?"

"Christ, you sure belted him."

"Well, he had it coming. If it wasn't me, it would be somebody else."

Mr. Majestyk finished his beer and wiped his mouth with a paper napkin. "What have you got to do?"

"I'm still clearing that frontage, all the driftwood and crap."

"Hey, we never figured your day off."

"I thought Saturday," Ryan said.

"Saturday's out. That's our busy day, people leaving, new people coming in. Tomorrow or Friday."

"Tomorrow's all right. I don't care."

"You got nothing to do, take a run up and see that

property. ROGERS, the sign says," Mr. Majestyk paused; he made a decision, and looked right at Ryan and said, "I see you got a car."

"It's just borrowed."

"I didn't think she gave it to you."

When Mr. Majestyk paused again, Ryan waited; he wasn't going to help him; if the guy wanted to stick his nose in, he'd have to think of a way to do it.

Finally Mr. Majestyk said, "That's the car she run the two guys off the road with."

"I figured," Ryan said, "from the dings in the front end."

"The one kid has got two broken legs and internal injuries."

"You told me."

"Long as you remember," Mr. Majestyk said. He dropped it there.

Ryan had a cigarette and stretched out in the sun for a half hour, then got going on the frontage again, raking out the tangled brush and crap and dragging it into a pile. He was burning it when Mr. Majestyk came grinding across the uneven ground in his bulldozer, a stubby yellow machine that Ryan figured must be the smallest one made, though, God, the diesel engine made a racket. Mr. Majestyk showed him the gears and how to raise and lower the blade and for the next couple of hours Ryan played with the bulldozer, gradually digging out a hollow to bury the junk in that wouldn't burn.

When the beer drinkers from No. 11 came down with the Scotch-Kooler, he knew it was after four, time to knock off. He'd bury the junk tomorrow. No, Friday. He was hot and sweaty from two and a half hours in the field; he was wearing just his cut-off khakis, so he walked out into the lake and swam to the raft and back. He wasn't a good swimmer; he had no endurance, but his form was good and it wasn't any harder than swimming out to the boat last night. That was funny, he hadn't thought about her all day. He thought about a beer and walked across the beach within ten feet of the beer drinkers ready to say "hi" if they

116

looked at him, but they were laughing at something and didn't seem to notice him.

"Hey, you got a phone call!" Mr. Majestyk was crossing in front of No. 1 from his house.

"Where?"

"No, a message. I told her you were working. She says to tell you six o'clock."

"She give you her name?"

Mr. Majestyk's solemn expression held on Ryan. "Maybe you're crazy, she isn't."

Ryan moved off. The hell with him and what he thought.

He was near the swimming pool when Virginia Murray came out of No. 5. He saw her waiting for him and there was nothing he could do about it.

"Hi—I thought you were going to fix my window."

She was in her aqua bathing suit. She had come in from the pool, had seen Ryan, had wiped the oil from her face, and gone out again.

"Hey, I forgot—no, I didn't forget, I just couldn't get to it today."

"Could you look at it now?"

Her figure was all right. Pretty good, in fact: nice bazooms, good legs, not too fat, but sunburned and sore-looking; over a week here and still sunburned.

"Listen, I would but I got to run. This person is waiting for me." He was moving away. "Tomorrow for sure, okay?" She was nodding as he turned and that was the end of it.

He turned off the Shore Road and followed the winding drive through the trees to Old Pointe Road, then crept along until he saw the new-looking white two-story house with the attached garage and well-kept shrubbery. The name on the mailbox, R. J. Ritchie, made him hesitate. He hadn't got a good look at this side of the house last night. They had come around through the trees and he had waited by the garage while Nancy went in for the wire. He turned into Ritchie's drive slowly.

"You're late, Jackie."

117

Her voice came from above. From one of the second-floor windows. He saw her now, leaning on the windowsill, looking down at him. "Walk in," she said. "The door's open." She was holding something in her hand. Ryan pulled close to the garage and stopped. Looking straight up now, he saw the gun. Nancy was pointing it at him.

ELEVEN

RYAN WENT FROM THE KITCHEN INTO THE living room, taking his time as he looked around, the appraiser getting the feel of the place: the white walls and the dark wood in the quiet of early evening, the hardwood floor and the Oriental rug and the iron stairway that came up out of the living room floor and curved once into the ceiling. The dining room, too, through the open doorway was white and dark with a heavy table and wrought iron things on the wall.

You would have to be a weight lifter to clean this place. He walked over to the den and looked in. It was paneled, stained a gray-green with canvas chairs and big blue and green ashtrays. He wasn't sure of the paintings; maybe they were all right, but he couldn't put a price on them. The color TV he could get a hundred and a half for. He came back into the living room to the sliding glass doors along the front wall. Below, out past the sun deck, he could see the swimming pool and the lawn. Standing closer to the glass, he could see part of the patio.

He turned as Nancy came down the stairs—brown legs and a straw purse, then tan shorts and sweater and her dark hair.

She said, "Did you go to the lodge?"

It came as a little shock feeling inside him that he hadn't gone out to look at Ray's hunting lodge, that he had forgotten all about it.

"I didn't have time."

She stared at him a moment and turned away.

"I got hung up with work," Ryan said, following Nancy down to the lower level, to the activities room bar, then through the sliding screen doors out to the patio. Ryan watched her drop the purse on the umbrella table.

"Is it loaded?"

She was facing him now, her cool look gone and smiling a little. "Of course it's loaded."

"What kind is it?"

"Twenty-two."

"You going to shoot something?"

"We could. Windows are good."

"We've done windows."

"Not with a gun."

"Have you?"

"Not in a while. Hey, are you hungry?"

"I guess so. Were the windows around here?"

"Uh-huh, when I first came up. I knew there wouldn't be anything to do."

"So you brought a gun to shoot at windows."

"And boats. Boats are fun."

"I imagine they would be. How about cars?"

"I didn't think about cars." She seemed pleasantly surprised. "Isn't that funny?"

"Yeah, that is funny."

"I just wanted you to know we have it."

"There's a difference," Ryan said, "between breaking and entering and armed robbery."

"And there's a difference between seventy-eight dollars and fifty thousand dollars," Nancy said. "How badly do you want it?"

The telephone rang in the activities room. Nancy's gaze held on Ryan; she was watching for his reaction. He showed nothing, keeping his eyes on hers, and she smiled a little and walked off.

When she was inside, Ryan took the long-barreled

target pistol out of her purse. He knew the kind; he'd sold them at the sporting goods store. He extended his arm, aiming and putting the front sight on the lamppost. He pulled the clip out of the polished hickory grip; it was loaded, all right. Then he shoved it back in and returned the gun to her purse.

He walked out by the swimming pool with his hands in his pockets, past the swimming pool and across the lawn. He could still feel the polished grip in his hand and the balanced weight of the gun. He saw himself pulling the gun out of his raincoat as he walked up to the cashier's window—not a bank, God no—a small loan company like the one Bud Long worked for, with two or three people behind the counter. As he pulled the gun Leon Woody would turn from where he was filling out a loan application and go over the counter and clean the place. They would have studied the place and timed it so that he'd walk in a few minutes before closing. Hit the place and then get out fast. They had talked about it once. Just once. Because it would be robbery, armed, and it could take all the nerve they had ever used during all the B & E's put together and it still might not be enough to go in with a gun.

He walked to the edge of the lawn, to the bluff that dropped steeply to the beach, down to all the sand and water. The boat was gone; the guy from the club must have come and picked it up.

It was quiet and the grass felt good. He turned and started back. It was a funny thing, he had never in his life cut grass. The lawn had been cut recently and it was better than any infield he had ever played on. You would have to play the ball different on grass like this; it would skid and take low hops. You'd have to get used to playing it and then it wouldn't be too bad.

Nancy was on the patio holding a tray, placing it on the umbrella table now and looking out toward him.

He felt all right but not completely at ease. It was a before-the-game feeling, or a walking-through-somebody's-house feeling. He wouldn't show it; he'd had enough practice not showing it; but he couldn't do anything about the feeling being there. The girl and the

120

swimming pool and the patio, but something was wrong. For some reason it wasn't as good as sitting in the Pier Bar at six o'clock with an ice cold beer and not having to think about anything.

"Beer or Cold Duck?" Nancy was waiting for him with two bottles of beer on the tray, a bottle of mixed Cold Duck, and a pasteboard bucket of fried chicken. "I phoned for it," Nancy said. "It isn't very good chicken, but I didn't imagine you'd be taking me out to dinner."

Ryan opened a beer and sat down in a canvas chair. He lit a cigarette and now he waited. But she outwaited him and he said, "Who was it? Ray?"

"Ray called this afternoon. It was Bob Junior," Nancy said. "He wants to come over."

"What did you tell him?"

"I told him I'm tired and I'm going to bed early. He said something clever and I told him if I saw his truck drive up, I'd call his wife."

"I don't get that," Ryan said, "going out with him."

"It was something to do." She was pouring a glass of Cold Duck at the table. "I guess to see if he had the nerve more than anything else."

"You've got a thing about nerve."

She turned with the glass in her hand. "What else is there? I mean, that you can count on."

"What if your nerve gets you in trouble? What if Ray finds out?"

"About Bob Junior?"

"Of if somebody tells him they saw us together."

Nancy shrugged, the little girl movement again. "I don't know. I'd think of something." She pulled a chair close to his and sat down. "Why all the questions? A little nervous, Charlie?"

"You said Ray called earlier."

"He won't be up until Saturday. He has to go to Cleveland."

"What does that mean?"

"It means he'll be in Cleveland and won't be here Friday night. How does that grab you?"

"But the money will."

121

"It has to be if they pay them Saturday." Nancy waited. "That's why I've decided we should sneak in the lodge tonight."

Ryan shook his head. "Not till I look at it in the day."

"You've seen it before."

"Not with this in mind."

"I've been thinking about it all day," Nancy said. "Sneaking in and going through it in the dark."

"Tomorrow's my day off," Ryan said. "I can go over sometime tomorrow."

"Okay, I'll go with you. Then we'll sneak in tomorrow night."

He wished he could ruffle her, shake her up a little. "It might not work," Ryan said. "You know there's that possibility."

"But we'll never know unless we try," Nancy said. "Will we?"

Ryan ate some of the chicken and with the second bottle of beer began to relax. But as he relaxed he became aware of something happening. Nancy sat next to him, facing him, a brown knee almost touching his chair. She would hold a piece of chicken in both hands and take little bites as she watched him. She would sip her wine and look at him over the rim of the glass. She would move her hair from her eye and let it fall back again. They ate in silence and he let it work on him. Sitting low in the chair and now lighting a cigarette, aware of the dark-haired girl close to him, giving him the business, and Ryan said to himself: You are being set up.

He was being offered the bait, shown what it would be like. He had been taken up on a high mountain by Ann-Margret and was being shown all the kingdoms of the world, all that could be his. While off from them, across clean tile, the underwater lights of the swimming pool glowed in the dusk.

How do you get that sure of yourself? Ryan thought. And then he thought, She makes it look easy.

She'll do it one time and get fifty grand and never know it's hard.

He could break into a place and Leon Woody could

122

break into a place and all kinds of other guys could break into places, most of the guys pretty dumb or strung out, but that didn't mean she could do it. It wasn't like throwing rocks and running, it wasn't a game; it was real and maybe she could do it without clutching up, but how did she know until she had done it and found out what it was like? That's what got him. If it was so easy, what did she need him for? Like he was some stiff she was hiring to do the heavy work. Like she could do it, but she didn't want to strain herself and get a hernia.

Ryan said, "If you were going to break into a place, how would you do it?"

Nancy thought a moment. "I'd try the door first."

"What if somebody's home?"

"Oh, I thought you meant the lodge."

"Anyplace, if you wanted to break in."

"I guess," Nancy said, "I'd still try the door." She smiled a little. "Very quietly."

"What if it's locked?"

"Then I'd try a window."

"And if the windows are locked."

"I don't know; I guess I'd break one."

"You know how to do that?"

"Hey, but in the summer you wouldn't have to," Nancy said. "You could just cut a hole in the screen."

"If there's a window open."

She sat up. "Let's do it. Break into somebody's house."

"What for? There's no reason."

"For fun."

And Leon Woody said, "Like, man, a game?" And he said to Leon Woody, riding along in the carpet cleaning truck, "Yeah, sort of a game."

Ryan said, "Have you ever done it?"

Nancy shook her head. "Not really."

"What do you mean, not really? You either have or you haven't."

"I've looked through people's houses when they weren't home."

"And you think it's fun."

"Uh-huh, don't you?"

And Leon Woody said, "Do you know what you get if you lose the game?" And he said to Leon Woody, "That's part of it. The risk."

"How do you know if you have the nerve?" Ryan said to her.

"Oh, come on." Nancy reached toward the umbrella table for a cigarette. "What's so hard about sneaking into a house?"

There.

Ryan waited. He watched her light the cigarette and exhale smoke to blow out the match. He waited until she looked at him and then he said, "Do you want to try it?"

"No rocks tonight," Ryan said. "Okay?"

"No rocks," Nancy said. "I've decided if there aren't any lights on, no one's home. It's dark enough but it's too early for people to be in bed."

"Maybe they're on the porch."

"Maybe," she said. "Of course where the lights are *on,* they might still not be home. I always leave a light on."

"I guess most people do."

"So we'll have to go up close and take a look."

She was at ease, Ryan could feel that. He couldn't imagine her not at ease. But she still could be faking it. It was still talking and not doing and there were a few miles of nerve between the two.

"Which house?" Ryan said.

"I was thinking that dark one."

"Let's go."

He would remember, after, that he'd said it. She didn't have to plead with him or push him. She stood relaxed, watching him, and when he said, "Let's go," she smiled —he would remember that too—and followed him across the beach, up into the tree darkness that closed in on the houses, out of the trees and across a front lawn and up the steps to the porch of the house that showed no lights, doing it now and not fooling around, hoping he was shaking her up a little.

Ryan pushed the doorbell.

"What do you say if someone comes?" Her voice was calm, above a whisper.

124

"We ask if they know where the Morrisons live."

"What if that's their name?"

He rang the bell again and waited, giving them enough time to come down if they were upstairs in bed. He waited another moment, putting it off, then opened the screen and tried the door. The knob turned in his hand.

"I told you it wasn't hard," Nancy said. She started past him into the house.

"Wait till I look."

He went in, through the darkness to the back of the house, to the kitchen, where he looked out the window and saw the rear end of the car in the garage. He moved back through the house.

Nancy was sitting on the porch rail smoking a cigarette. He took it from her to throw it away, but he saw the way she was looking at him and he took a drag on the cigarette and handed it back to her.

"Well?"

"They're close by. They won't be gone long."

"How do you know?"

"I just know. Okay?"

She shrugged, standing up. He saw the movement and maybe a faint smile, though in the dark he wasn't sure of the smile. She came down the steps after him and they crossed the lawn to the beach.

"If the car's there," Ryan said. "they're not far away."

"I've been thinking, Jackie. If we go in where we know they're not home, what's the fun?"

Ryan stared at her and he heard Leon Woody say, "You go in when they're *not* home, when you know it and have it in writing they're not home."

He kept looking at her until she was about to say something, until he said, "Come on," and they went up from the beach into the trees again, moving in on the house closest to them that showed lights, running hunch-shouldered—the same way they had gone in to throw the rocks—keeping to the trees and bushes and deep shadows until they were next to the house and could edge up to a window and look in.

"Playing cards," Ryan said.

"Gin. She just went down and he's mad."

125

"Come on."

There wasn't anything to see. There wouldn't be, either, Ryan was sure of that. Not when you were expecting something. Like the carpet cleaning job, expecting to see the broads going around without any clothes on. They moved along the beach front from one house to the next. They saw people playing gin, people reading, people watching television, people eating, people drinking, people talking, and more people drinking.

"Maybe we'll catch somebody in bed," Nancy said.

"If they're in bed, they'll have the lights off."

"Not everybody."

"Would you like somebody watching you?"

"I've never thought of it," Nancy said.

They saw people playing bridge and people sitting, not doing anything. They saw a woman alone, reading, and Nancy drew her fingernail down the screen. The woman jumped visibly and sat staring at the window, afraid to move.

When they were in the trees again, Ryan said, "That was fun. Maybe we can find some old lady with heart trouble."

Ryan didn't recognize the brown house when they came to it. If they had come up from the beach, he would have, even in the dark. He knew the house was along here, but he wasn't looking for it and by the time they were across the side yard and to the porch, he was too close to the house to recognize it.

They moved around the far side, past dark windows, and came to the back porch and he still didn't recognize the house. He was watching Nancy now as she walked out to the garage and looked in.

As she reached him she said, "There's no car in the garage, but let's go in anyway."

Both the front and back doors were locked, but it was still easy. They went in through a living room window off the porch after Ryan poked a hole in the screen with a stick and flicked open the latch; Ryan first and then Nancy. She followed him to the front hall and stood close while he checked the back door, opening it and closing it

126

quietly, feeling better now with a way to go out on three sides of the house.

The light, throwing a shadow on the wall, startled him, turning him from the door.

Nancy had opened the refrigerator.

"Beer?" She was hunched over, looking in, offering him a can of beer behind her back. "They don't have a whole lot to offer."

"They didn't know we were coming," Ryan said. He popped open the top and took a good swallow of the beer.

"Salad dressing, mustard, milk, pickles, jelly, mustard —they've got enough mustard, God—four jars, and cat-sup—two, three—they must live on mustard and catsup."

"Maybe they had a party."

As he said it, moving toward the doorway to the hall, he knew where they were and was sure of it even before he stepped into the hall and saw the stairway on the right and the faint outside light coming from the two windows on the landing.

"Kitchens aren't much," Nancy said. She was behind him now. "I like bedrooms the best."

It was funny being here. At first, realizing where he was gave him an uneasy, on-guard feeling, as if something were wrong. But it was all right. So it was the same house. It could be the one next door or down the beach; it was a house. Going into it again didn't mean a thing. Right? And Leon Woody would say, "Right, man, it don't mean anything. You just walk in the same house and don't know it." But kidding. He wouldn't really mean it.

They went up the stairs holding the rail, Ryan still in front. At the top he stopped a moment to listen, then went into the first bedroom on the right, the one where he and Billy Ruiz had found the men's clothes. The room was familiar: the window over the back porch, the dresser, the twin beds, the night table where he had put his cigar. He remembered now that he must have left the cigar in the ashtray and he moved between the beds to see if it was still there, not expecting to find it but cu-

127

rious. Nancy went past him to the dresser and began going through the drawers.

Ryan sat on the bed, sipping his beer, watching her. She had opened a drawer and was feeling inside, closing it gently now and opening the next drawer to dig her hands under the clothes and feeling around in there thoroughly. "You see, what she does she goes through everything to make sure no valuables are hidden anywhere." And Leon Woody would say, "Yeah, the valuables. Say, man, did you tell her about dumping the drawers on the floor to get at all them valuables?"

No, he didn't tell her about that. He finished the beer and went through the bath to the adjoining bedroom, the one the women had used Sunday, and checked the tops of the dresser and the chest of drawers. There were two more bedrooms across the hall. He looked into each but saw nothing worth taking, not a hundred and fifty miles from Detroit without a car. He thought of something then and went back through the second bedroom to the bath and opened the medicine cabinet. The Jade East was still there. He rubbed a few drops of the lotion between his palms, then over his jaw, staring at the mirror but barely making out his reflection in the darkness.

He went into the bedroom where he had left Nancy— not hearing a sound in the room and not seeing her at first because he expected to see her standing by the dresser or by the closet. He looked toward the door and as his gaze shifted he saw the movement on the bed, *in* the bed, that's where she was, in bed with the spread pulled up to her chin. She was watching him, waiting for him to find her, watching him now as he came around between the twin beds and sat down on the empty one.

"I give up," Ryan said. "What're you doing?"

"Waiting for you," she said, giving him the look with her dark hair on the white pillow. "Guess if I have any clothes on."

"You're kidding."

"Guess."

He began to nod then, slowly, "You would, wouldn't you?"

128

"You're right," Nancy said. "Know what you win?"

"Listen, I know a better place."

"Where?"

"My room."

"Nope. Right here."

"Why?"

"I don't think it's ever been done before."

"I believe it and I'll tell you why," Ryan said.

"In other people's houses after you've sneaked in. That's the new game."

"I've heard it's not as much fun, listening for somebody to walk in."

Nancy smiled. "Wouldn't that be good? Can you see the look on their face?"

"Just tell me why," Ryan said. "Okay?"

"Why. That's all you say. You know, Jackie, you're really sort of a drag. I thought you might be fun, but I don't know——"

"Move over."

"First you have to take off your clothes. It's a rule."

"Shoes?"

"Everything."

He began unbuttoning his shirt and pulling out the tails, standing close to the bed now and looking down at her.

"Everything," Nancy said.

"In a minute." Ryan eased down next to her and her hands held the spread tightly up under her chin.

"Not till everything's off."

He leaned in closer, placing his hands on the pillow so that she was looking directly up at him now, between his arms.

She sniffed. "What's that?"

"Nice?"

"You put too much on."

"You want to talk or what?"

"I told you the rule——"

He leaned in almost all the way, setting the angle so that their mouths would fit just right and feeling her strain a little toward him, and there he hesitated, holding motionless.

129

Almost touching his mouth she said, "What's the matter?"

"Shhh."

Neither of them moved. The room, the house, was silent.

"I didn't hear anything."

Ryan pushed himself up slowly, bringing his hands off the pillow. He touched a finger to his mouth as he rose and moved quietly around the bed to the door. He stood with one hand on the doorframe, leaning into the hall, listening. He glanced at her and now he was moving, closing the door and locking it carefully, stepping to the window to look out, hesitating, then pushing open the screen and lowering it to the porch roof. Going out the window, ducking under, he looked at her once more.

"You going to wait for them?"

"Where are they?"

He motioned with one hand, pointing down to the floor. "Come on."

Then he was out, over the edge of the roof and hanging a moment before dropping. He was in the field bordering the yard, in the high brush, before he turned to see Nancy coming out the window, fully dressed. She stood looking down, undecided, and Ryan smiled. He waited patiently, knowing she would come down because she had no choice, and right now seconds to her were like minutes. He watched her go to her knees and look down again and slowly roll over and let the lower part of her body hang from the roof. It's going to sting your feet, Ryan thought, but it's the only way. He watched her drop and stumble and stand motionless as she came to her feet.

From the edge of the bushes he called softly, "Hey!" and waited for her to reach him. He took her arm then and moved through the brush and scrub trees toward the beach, almost running, dragging her after him. As he reached the low rise above the sand he turned to catch her, letting her weight and momentum carry them over the edge so that they fell down to the sand clinging to each other, rolling and coming to a stop with Ryan lying partly on top of her, one leg over hers, resting his weight on his arms beneath her. He could feel her breathing

130

against him as she tried to catch her breath, the nice nose and the partly open mouth close to his face and her eyes closed. He waited until her eyes opened, then waited a little more, looking at her and feeling her body relax.

"You get dressed quick."

Her expression was calm, but her gaze held his expectantly, sensing something in his eyes or in the tone of his voice.

"You didn't hear anyone," she said finally. "You didn't hear a thing."

"Just for a while," Ryan said, "let's not talk, okay?"

"If we're going to not talk," Nancy said, "I'd rather not talk somewhere else."

"You don't like the sand?"

"I'm not the outdoorsy type, Jackie. You might as well know it."

"I don't think I can move."

"Try," Nancy said.

Ryan watched himself at certain times, sometimes when he was alone—like standing seven feet off third base and his hat on just right, or walking along the beach or driving a car—but usually it happened when he was with certain people. He wasn't aware of himself when he was with Mr. Majestyk. But he was aware of himself almost all the time with Nancy, seeing himself and hearing himself and most of the time he looked dumb. Big jerky dumb guy saying dumb things, trying to impress the girl. He couldn't get in the right frame of mind to feel sure of himself. He could fake it; he could act like the big smooth-o; but he could feel her watching him, still not impressed, maybe laughing at him, and he never for more than a moment felt in control. He was pretty sure she was at ease. But what if she was faking it? What if she was someone else inside, the way she said her mother was someone else looking out through her eyes? Maybe she was faking it. She was being cool and he was being cool, each trying to be cooler than the other until pretty soon, Ryan decided, you get so cool you can't even move because of the chance that anything at all you might do might turn out to be dumb—anything. What good was being cool if you weren't you? Whoever *you* are, Ryan thought.

He was at the wheel, aware of himself acting natural, not telling her where they were going and finally not having to tell her as they pulled in past the big blue-lit Bay Vista sign with the small red NO VACANCY glowing beneath it.

"I'll show you where I live."

He got out and waited for her and finally she came with him, around the side of the motel to his room.

"Wow," Nancy said. She stood looking toward the dark swimming pool and the closed-in area between the cabanas that extended out to the beach.

"What's the matter?"

"I can just see everybody at the pool," Nancy said.

"All the tool and die makers sitting around in their vacation outfits."

"Some of them go down to the beach."

"That'd be fun too. Like a Black Sea resort."

He opened the door to No. 7 and she stood just inside, looking around. Ryan had to move her to close the door. Then he stood looking around with her.

"Yes, it certainly is nice."

"It's all right," Ryan said. "The bed's comfortable. The walls could use some paint. I don't know as I'll bother, though."

"Just hang some pictures."

"I could do that, hang some pictures. Cover up where it's peeling."

"Get some of those nice old master prints at the dime store."

"They have them there?"

"God, you probably would."

"Well, to cover up the bad spots."

"What else do you want to show me?"

"That's all. I just wanted to show you where I live."

"Great," Nancy said. She turned to the door.

"I thought we might just sit around here," Ryan said. "Or lie around."

Ryan smiled.

"Show me the rest first," Nancy said.

Outside again she stood looking toward the swimming pool and the trees and the lights showing in the windows of the cabanas.

"The place really jumps, doesn't it?"

"A lot of families are here. With kids."

"Oh," Nancy said, "with kids. That should be fun."

She walked out to the pool, Ryan following. She stood at the edge looking into the water. A few steps behind her, watching her, Ryan thought: Boot her in the ass and go get a beer.

And what would that prove?

Well, it might not prove anything, but it was a thought. He could hear sounds now from No. 11, the beer drinkers, their wall of cans showing faintly in the darkness. He looked around. There was a light on in No. 5 behind the closed drapes. No. 5, the broad with the window. Or whatever her game was. He could go over right now and knock on the door and say, "Let's see the window, honey," catching her off-guard, and she'd probably say, "What window?"

"I'm sorry," Nancy said.

He could feel her close behind him and could picture her waiting for him to turn around, the good little dark-haired girl waiting patiently, throwing it at him softly and getting him off-stride again, like a goddamn change-up.

"What're you sorry about?" He half turned as he said it.

"I don't know. I have the feeling you're mad at me."

"I'm not mad."

"I just didn't feel like staying inside."

"Well, you said you're not the outdoor type."

"Outdoorsy, I said. I'm just not in the mood." She edged a little to the side to work around in front of him. "I think I'll be in the mood later. All right?"

"I sure appreciate it."

"Don't be mad. Let's do something."

"Yeah, well, if you bust any windows around here, you know who has to fix them."

"That's better." She was smiling at him. "No—let's just look around."

"At the dumb families and the dumb kids?"

She reached up, taking his face between her hands, stretching up against him and pulling his face down; she kissed his mouth lightly and quietly, moving around a little but staying right in there and applying pressure when his arms went around her and his hands spread over her back.

She took his hand. "Come on, show me the Bay Villa."

"Vista."

"All right, then show me the Bay Vista."

They were walking toward the beach now, holding hands, Ryan standing off from them watching them and glad it was dark.

"This is all there is to it. Fourteen cabanas——"

"Cabanas?"

"That's what he calls them. And the motel."

"Who's he?"

"Mr. Majestyk."

"Oh, the one you were with at the Pier?"

"That's right."

"Where does he live?"

"In a house. Around the other side of Number One."

"Show me."

"It's just a house."

A beam of light spread out from the bole of a fir tree to flood Mr. Majestyk's garden, illuminating the neatly trimmed shrubbery and border of white-painted rocks, the pale clean trunks of birch trees, the pair of flamingoes feeding beneath the birdhouse.

"Beautiful," Nancy whispered. They were crossing the lawn in the darkness beyond the spotlight.

"He's home," Ryan said. "He's probably watching television."

"I'm sure he is," Nancy said. "I love the lamp in the window."

"His daughter decorated the place for him."

"I want to see it."

They were nearing the far edge of the lawn and now Nancy started toward the house, approaching the dark side that faced the empty field. A window was open, showing a square of rose-colored light through the screen.

Ryan caught her arm. "The door's on the other side."

"I don't want to go *in*."

She pulled away from him and there was nothing he could do but follow her to the window. He stood next to her, against the wall, as she looked in.

Mr. Majestyk was in his reclining chair facing the television set. He was watching a Western movie, watching intently, with a can of beer and a cigar. He would lean forward to take a sip of beer, his eyes holding on the screen, and the back of the Recline-O-Rama chair would rise with him, following him to an upright position. Dragging on the cigar, he would lean back again, pushing, bumping hard against the chair, and both Mr. Majestyk and the chair would settle back again.

"Wow," Nancy said.

Ryan could hear the movie dialogue, a familiar voice, a quiet, Western drawl, then a woman's voice. He recognized the drawl; he knew it right away. He edged close to the window and looked in, across the room, past Mr. Majestyk to Randolph Scott in the good hat that was curled just right in front. He couldn't remember who the woman was, not bad-looking but sort of old. She sounded tired, like she had given up, saying she didn't care what happened to her. Then Randolph Scott saying, "When you get done feeling sorry for yourself, I'll tell you something . . . you're alive and he's dead and that makes the difference."

"I love purple and silver," Nancy whispered. "And lavender."

He had seen the picture before. He remembered it now, a good one. Richard Boone was the bad guy. He and a couple of others hold up the stage and take Randolph and the woman and her husband prisoner, holding them for ransom because the woman's dad was rich. The husband's a coward and gets shot and you know they're going to shoot Randolph and the woman once they get the dough, unless Randolph does something.

"The pictures," Nancy said. "Those are the authentic dime store reproductions I was telling you about."

"Shhh."

"With white imitation antiqued frames. Beautiful."

Mr. Majestyk and his chair sat up. He twisted around,

135

looking over his shoulder, listening, and they ducked away from the window.

There was silence. Ryan stood in the dark with his back to the wall. He heard horses inside, the sound of their hooves fading away. There was no music or dialogue now. Something was about to happen. Maybe the part where Randolph goes in the cave after the guy named Billy Jack—that was a good part—the guy in there after the woman while his buddies are away. Randolph sneaks up behind Billy Jack and is about to belt him when Billy Jack turns and you think right away there's going to be a fight; but, no, Randolph jams the sawed-off shotgun under Billy Jack's chin and *wham* the guy's face disappears quick, the way it would happen, without one of those fakey fights.

Nancy was looking in the window again. "Beautiful," she whispered and giggled.

"Let's go," Ryan said.

"Just a minute."

"He's going to hear you."

Wham, the shotgun went off and Ryan looked in. Yeah, that was the part. Randolph had the sawed-off shotgun now and the babe was holding her hands over her mouth, probably wetting her pants.

"God, where do you suppose he buys his furniture?"

"Come on, let's go."

"You have to see it to believe it. The lamp in the picture window——"

"Come on."

"——with the cellophane on the shade. Hey, did you hear the one—do you know who won the Polish beauty contest?"

Ryan shook his head, pretending to be patient, letting her talk.

"Nobody," Nancy said.

She laughed out loud and Mr. Majestyk twisted around in the chair, rolling out of it as the back popped straight up. He started for the window but turned abruptly and hurried across the room and through the double doors to the porch.

136

"He's coming," Ryan said. On the other side of the house the screen door slammed.

Nancy was looking in the window again. "You're right. I think it's time to cut."

"Wait a minute——"

Before he could reach out for her, she was across the narrow space of lawn and into the field, into the darkness of the heavy brush, out of sight. For a moment he could follow her sound. He wanted to get out of there quick, go after her. But he hesitated. He waited. When he moved off, it was around to the front of the house. Mr. Majestyk was coming through the illuminated garden, past the two flamingoes.

"Hey, was that you?"

"What?"

"Somebody laughing."

"What do you mean?" Ryan said.

"I mean, somebody laughing. What do you think I mean?"

"Maybe somebody on the beach."

"Christ, it was like right outside the window."

"I don't know, I didn't hear anything."

Mr. Majestyk was staring at him. "You come around from that side, you didn't hear anything?"

"I was taking a walk."

"You can't hear when you're walking?"

"I didn't *hear* anything. How many times I have to tell you?"

"You didn't see a girl? It sounded like a broad laughing."

"I didn't see any girl or anybody."

"I don't know," Mr. Majestyk said. "Maybe it's me. Maybe I should get my goddamn ears checked." That seemed to end it. Mr. Majestyk paused, about to turn and go back inside. He looked at Ryan again. "Hey, you want to see a good movie?"

"I saw it," Ryan said.

As he heard himself and saw Mr. Majestyk frown he wanted to keep talking, but there wasn't anything to say and a little silence hung there between them.

"How do you know you saw it?"

"I was walking by, I heard the TV. I remembered, you know, it sounded familiar. What they were saying. It's a Western, isn't it? Randolph Scott?"

"You hear a TV inside somebody's house," Mr. Majestyk said, "but you don't hear somebody laughing *out*side, right where you're at?"

"I didn't hear anybody. You want me to write it down and sign it, for Christ sake?"

"Take it easy."

"Your ass, take it easy. You believe me or not?"

"Forget it."

"I don't forget it, you're calling me a liar and I don't like it."

"Hey, come on—I haven't called you anything."

Ryan stood facing him. "You believe me or not?"

"Okay, I believe you," Mr. Majestyk said. "You want me to write it down and sign it?"

"Forget it," Ryan said. He walked past Mr. Majestyk, out of the light into darkness.

If Jackie didn't follow her the beach way, Nancy decided, he would come over in the car, race over to arrive before she did, and be waiting with some nifty remark like, "Where you been?" From then on all his moves would be toward the bedroom. Naturally. If a girl asked you to steal $50,000 with her, she wasn't going to say no to falling into bed, for God sake. Ryan would think that way and there was no reason he shouldn't. Nancy looked at it as part of the plot, the romantic portion of The Great Cucumber Payroll Robbery. Or, Nancy and Jack at the Seashore. Though it was really a lake. Or, Two Mixed-Up Kids Trying to Make Out. They would make out. Nancy was reasonably sure of that. But if anything did happen, Ryan would be left with the bag and she would deny, if she had to, ever having seen him before. That part, if it ever happened, would be called Tough Bananas, Charlie. Or, Some You Win and Some You Lose.

It would be too bad if it happened, because she liked Jack Ryan. She liked his looks. She liked his face and his eyes and the smooth, tan leanness of him. She liked the way he stood with his hands on his hips, a little phony but not too phony. She liked the quiet way he talked and some of the dry things he said. It was too bad Jack wasn't Ray. If Jack Ryan were Ray Ritchie, the whole view of her situation would be different. It didn't mean she would stay with Ryan forever, she would have to think about the future; but at least the present would be more fun. It really was too bad Jack wasn't Ray. It was too bad all the Ryans and the Ritchies in the world couldn't trade places.

When she got home, she would turn on one lamp and the record player and watch Jackie lead up to it. He would probably be very quiet and move slowly but not waste much time, either. Maybe they should go for a swim first, with nothing on: the ultimate test of how poised he really was.

Nancy climbed the stairs to the front lawn. The pool did look sexy with the underwater lights turning the water green. If she knew for sure he was here watching, she could give him a little preview before the main feature. There were no lights on in the living room. Of course not, he'd be sitting on the couch in the dark, with a good view of the front lawn and the pool, going over his nifty remark and the way he'd say it. He could be watching her right now.

He *was* watching her; she could feel it.

Nancy walked to the edge of the pool. She took off her sneakers and dipped one foot into the water. She peeled off the tan sweater and shook her hair. She unbuttoned her blouse and felt the water again with her toes, taking her time. He would be on the edge of the couch now. As she took the blouse off he would see she wasn't wearing a bra and that would bring him out of his seat. Okay, Jackie, Nancy thought, get ready. She unbuttoned her shorts and peeled to bare hips. Give him a little, Nancy thought. She turned slowly toward the house with her hands on her hips. She turned back, just as slowly, and dove in.

She swam across the pool underwater, came up, went down again, and pushed off against the side. In the middle of the pool she came to the surface and swam to the deep end with slow, easy strokes. To the shallow end and back would give him time to come down to the pool. She made her turn and stroked leisurely toward the diving board and now saw the figure coming out from the house, out of the deep shadow of the patio. She dove underwater, giving him time to reach the edge, and came up breaking the water smoothly, seeing the beer case he was carrying at his side, wondering why he had brought out a whole case of beer and realizing in the same moment that it wasn't Jack Ryan, that it was a man she had never seen before, a dark figure standing now at the edge of darkness, the lights of the swimming pool reflecting on his sunglasses.

"Hey, come out of there." Frank Pizarro grinned. "I got something for you."

Nancy stared up at him, one hand on the pool edge. "Get out," she said.

"Listen, don't yell or scream or nothing, okay?"

"Mr. Ritchie has private police who come by here and I think it's just about time——"

"They come see you swimming like that, uh? Goddamn," Pizarro said. "I don't blame them."

"Tell me what you want," Nancy said. "And then leave."

"I got something to sell you."

"You're trespassing," Nancy said. "You're wasting your time and mine and if you're still here when the police come, you're going to have a very hard time explaining it. They'll arrest you and put you in jail without asking questions. Just your being here will be enough to convict you."

Pizarro waited patiently. "It's wallets," he said.

"What?"

"It's wallets. I got some wallets I sell you for five hunnert dollar."

Nancy hesitated. He could be high on something or he could be psycho. She said quietly, "I don't need a wallet, so will you go, please?"

Pizarro shrugged. "It's okay. You don't want these wallets, then I got to take them to the goddamn police." He set the beer case close to the edge and kneeled on it, hunching down closer to her. "These wallets come from a place that was robbed. You understand?"

She had decided there was no sense in trying to understand him; but she wasn't sure what to say to threaten him, to make him leave. She said, "Yes, you should take them to the police. They'll appreciate your help."

"Sure," Pizarro said, "I can tell them who stole the wallets. Or I can leave the case somewhere the police will find it. With the name of the person written down inside." Pizarro watched her. "You know what I mean?"

"I know the private police should be here any minute——"

"Hey," Pizarro said. "No more bullshit about the private police, all right? I been here three hours waiting and this private police you got never come by." Pizarro grinned, trying to see her clearly through the distortion of the water. "Come out of there, okay," he said. "So I can tell you something."

TWELVE

VIRGINIA MURRAY WISHED THE WIRE OR whatever it was in the bra didn't dig into her chest the way it did. She loved the aqua bathing suit. It was neat with the white buttons down the front; it made her look trim. But it was so darned uncomfortable. The edge of the bra support, which curved beneath her right arm, dug in and left a welt you could feel. (The first time she felt it, the first day here, she was scared to death, because when her fingers touched the welt, she thought it was a lump in her breast.) The trouble was, the only other bathing suit she had was the green and yellow print, and with the skirt effect it made her look hippy.

She had already eaten breakfast. She had written to her mother and dad: "Can't believe it's Thursday already and almost time to come home. The past two weeks have gone by so fast. Whew! Will leave Saturday morning about ten or so (no hurry) and should be home before two. I miss both of you very much."

She had combed out her hair, put on the aqua bathing suit, and combed her hair again. She had taken her position on the studio couch to watch the morning begin and had looked through the new *Cosmopolitan,* which, she had a feeling, was getting awfully sexy lately.

Virginia was surprised when Mr. Majestyk came out to skim the pool instead of Jack Ryan. It was the first morning this week he had not come out about 9:15 or 9:20 with the aluminum pole.

He was probably doing something else. Perhaps raking the beach.

She could walk down to the beach, but if she did, she would have to stay at least for a short while and she didn't like to lie in the sand, even on a beach towel. It was too hot and she would feel herself perspire. It was strange, though, she had pictured herself with Jack Ryan on the beach. Yes, because she pictured them alone. It was late afternoon and she was lying on her back with her eyes closed beneath her sunglasses, very tan, with the straps of the aqua bathing suit unfastened and off her shoulders. She felt someone near her, she sensed it, and opened her eyes to see Jack Ryan standing over her. She looked up at him calmly, past the muscular curve of his naked chest. Finally he said, "Do you mind if I join you?" She told him please do. He dropped to his knees and she sat up, holding the front of her bathing suit against her chest. While they talked about nothing in particular she could feel that he wanted to tell her something. After a while they swam out into Lake Huron together, side by side, stroke for stroke; out about a half mile they rested and came back in.

They would take her car and go down the beach to a restaurant that looked out over the water and have broiled lake trout and white wine and watch the sun go down. On the way home he would try to tell her. He would sound awkward because he had never tried to express the way he felt. He had never met a girl like her. The girls he knew were out for whatever they could get. But she was different. She was, well, kind. Nice. No, not just nice, more than that. She made him feel, you know, *good*. Virginia would smile, not laughing at him, but warmly and say, "That's kind of you, but, really, I'm a very normal everyday sort of girl with no special talents or desires." He would say, "Well, what is it, then?" And she would say, "Perhaps the secret is that I see goodness in people, which is really God's love, you know, something everyone can discover in himself"—smiling then a little sadly—"if he would only take the time to look."

She wasn't sure what would happen after that.

But, darn it, she was sure of one thing—pulling at the bra where it dug into the side of her chest—she was going to take off the aqua suit and put on the green and yellow print and be comfortable for a change, even if it did make her look hippy.

She went into the bathroom. The green and yellow print was on one of the two outside door hooks, hanging next to her terry cloth robe. The door was a good idea: you could come right into the bathroom from outside without tracking sand all over the house; but you also had to be sure it was kept locked.

Virginia stepped out of the aqua suit. Turning to the door, she saw her reflection briefly in the medicine cabinet mirror. She picked up the aqua suit, glancing at the mirror again. The knock came as she was reaching for the green and yellow suit, as she stood naked by the door with the aqua suit in her other hand—several knocks in quick succession close to her, not two feet from where she was standing.

Ryan drove into Geneva Beach for breakfast.

After walking away from Mr. Majestyk last night, he had gone to his room to wait for Nancy. The car was here and he couldn't picture her walking home. So he lay on the bed to wait and read an article in *True* about a guy in Norwich, England, who had hooked, played, boated, and released more than two thousand pike in 15 years. When he realized Nancy wasn't coming, he thought about driving over to her house. But if Mr. Majestyk was still hanging around, he'd seen him or hear him drive off and know where he was going, because Mr. Majestyk knew the car. Then Mr. Majestyk might add it up and decide she was the girl he'd heard outside his window. Maybe it didn't matter. But why give the guy anything to think about? Parking the car in front of the Bay Vista had been dumb to begin with. He could have left it there and walked down to her house, but he'd see her tomorrow, all day. There was a good article in *True* about how Early Wynn used to dust batters and once even knocked his own kid down when the kid hit a long ball off him in batting practice. He read it and fell asleep.

At Estelle's he ordered eggs over easy and sausage and a glass of milk, then had coffee while he looked at the sports page of the *Free Press*. The Tigers were playing Washington tonight. Boston tomorrow night to open a five-game series. He hadn't seen a game yet this year. He hadn't even seen more than a few innings on television.

Maybe they could watch the game tonight, if it was on. He couldn't picture Nancy watching it, but maybe she wouldn't care if he did.

The plan for today was to drive by Ray's hunting lodge, look it over, and tonight go in, setting it up for Friday night. Looking it over wouldn't take long. They could spend the day at her place. He could bring beer and the wine she liked and a couple of steaks and they could play house most of the afternoon. It was too early to pick her up now. She probably slept late.

Back at the Bay Vista after breakfast, Ryan didn't know what to do. He didn't want to hang around and maybe run into Mr. Majestyk and he didn't want to sit in his room and read. For some reason he thought of the broad in No. 5, who was supposed to have the stuck window.

Virginia Murray didn't move. She wanted to. She wanted to back away from the door, or reach the terry cloth robe and put it on without touching the door. But what if she made a noise? She should have said some-

144

thing right away. "Just a minute." Or, "Who is it?" Then she could move around all she wanted. But now it was too late.

The succession of knocks came again, loud and startling, and she could see the edge of the door vibrate. Then silence. As it lengthened, Virginia began to relax. This was silly. She would simply wait for whoever it was to go away. They weren't going to stand there forever. But as she saw the knob turned and jiggled she jumped and heard her own voice before she realized she had cried out.

"What do you want?"

There was a moment's hesitation. "I come to fix your window."

She had to say something. "Can you come back later?"

"It's my day off. I only got a little while."

"Just a minute, please."

Virginia put on the terry cloth robe, hurrying but trying to be quiet and calm about it. She tied the sash and looked in the mirror, pulling the lapels closer together; but when she took her hand away, the lapels came apart. She hurried into the bedroom, taking off the robe, and immediately was sorry she had taken it off, feeling herself naked and picturing him outside waiting. If she took too long, he would know she had been standing in the bathroom without any clothes on. She had to hurry. She had to think. (Mother of God, help me!) She had to put something on. Something. Virginia reached into the closet. She pulled a dress from its hanger. Her light blue shift. My God, it was too thin. But she was going to wear it, because it was in her hand, because it was unzipped and she was stepping into it and zipping it up again, almost all the way up, smoothing the dress over her hips and glancing in the mirror. She was amazed. She looked fine; she even looked calm.

It was not until she was opening the door that she realized she was barefoot.

"You said you had a window was stuck?"

"Yes, come in, please." She hesitated. "It's in the bedroom."

Ryan was carrying the metal toolbox. Closing the door

145

behind him, he saw her aqua bathing suit lying open on the floor. He saw she wasn't wearing shoes with a dress on, and had to think about that one as he followed Virginia into the bedroom. He saw her stoop quickly next to the bed to pick up something and saw the way the dress stretched tightly but softly over her behind and smoothly across her back without the little ridge that brassiere fasteners make. By the time Virginia had raised the shade, standing against the morning sunlight coming in, Ryan knew damn well she didn't have anything on under the dress.

He put the toolbox on the floor. "Let me have a look."

Virginia was trying to raise the window, demonstrating, proving it wouldn't open. Ryan reached in past her. She jerked her arm out of the way, hitting her hand on the windowsill, and the bunched-up ball of white she was holding fell to the floor. Ryan looked down at her pants covering the toe of his right foot.

He looked up now at her face. Not too bad. Good skin. Greenish eyes. A nice smell—some kind of lotion. A very clean-looking broad. And a funny look in her eyes like she was really keyed up and ready, a broad who'd been here by herself almost two weeks, about twenty-seven, probably married—not the best-looking broad in the world, but she was a real living person and she had gone to a lot of trouble.

Ryan put his hands on her shoulders and began turning her away from the window. She kept staring at him with the funny look, her eyes wide open. He moved in closer, his hands sliding down her arms and then working around her waist to her back and pulling her against him; and when it felt just right, he pressed his mouth against hers and threw both of them across the bed.

At first he didn't realize she was struggling. He thought she was thrashing around, playing it up, but then, still kissing her, pressed against her, he opened his eyes and saw her eye like a giant eye fixed on him, an all-seeing eye looking into him—and filled with terror.

No, that wasn't it. It was a frantic look, a way-up-there look.

He nuzzled in, kissing her lightly about the mouth and

cheek, giving her the old Jack Ryan Special and moving his hand over her hip and up under her arm.

Very sloftly, barely taking his mouth from hers, he said, "Close your eyes." He kissed her cheek. Her eyes closed and opened and closed again and he kissed her eyelids, came down her nose and fooled around a little at the corner of her mouth and then on her lower lip, the old left hand working up there again under her arm, the cushion of his thumb moving in closer, yes, just starting to touch—and she jumped, she winced, opening her eyes.

Still softly, close, holding on, Ryan said, "What's the matter?"

"I have a little sore there," Virginia murmured. She sounded half asleep, drugged.

"A sore?"

"From my bathing suit. It rubs."

"Aww, I'm sorry." He eased his hand away, working it across her back, his fingers touching gently until he found the zipper of her dress. He began pulling it down and could feel her bare skin as it came open. She didn't seem aware of what he was doing until her dress was open to her waist. His hand went in to rest on the curve of her hip and her eyes, inches away from him, snapped open.

"Don't."

"Don't what?"

She didn't speak. She didn't move. She kept staring at him.

"Did I hurt you again?"

"Please don't."

"Don't what?"

She kept looking at him.

"Just tell me why not?" Ryan whispered, gentle and patient.

Her voice was low, but very clearly she said, "Because it's a sin."

"What do you mean, a sin?"

"It's a sin."

"A sin—what are we doing?"

"You know what we're doing," Virginia said.

"It's natural. I mean it's the way we are——"

"If you're married," Virginia Murray said.

147

"We're just fooling around." Ryan smiled at her.

"To me it's a sin." Virginia hesitated before adding, in a hushed tone, "I'm a Catholic."

"Well, that's all right," Ryan said. "So am I."

"You are not."

"I am. Honest to God."

"Say the Apostles' Creed."

"Aw, come on."

"If you're a Catholic, you know the Apostles' Creed."

"O my God I'm heartily sorry——"

"That's the Act of Contrition!"

"I believe in God, the Father Almighty," Ryan said, "Creator of heaven and earth—come on, what is this?"

"Will you get off me, please?"

"For Christ sake, you started it."

"Please don't use that language."

"You parade around without any pants on."

Virginia pulled away from him, turning out of his arms, and put her hands over her face. Her hands muffled the words as she said, "Please leave."

"What?"

"Leave!"

"God, you think I'm going to stay?" Ryan pushed up from the bed and straightened his pants. "I think," Ryan said, "you ought to make up your mind, that's all."

"I thought you'd come back last night," Nancy said.

Ryan was driving the Mustang. He glanced at her and brought his gaze back to the road. They had passed through Geneva Beach and were coming out on the highway south, out of tree shade into open sunlight. "I wanted to," Ryan said, "but he was still hanging around."

"So?"

"I mean he was watching."

"So what if he was?"

"I didn't want him asking any questions."

"Are you afraid of him?"

Ryan glanced at her again. "No, I'm not afraid of him—why should I be afraid?"

"I love his house," Nancy said. "God."

"He likes it."

"He's the justice of the peace," Nancy said. "Did you know that?"

"He told me you're going to appear in his court."

"I can hardly wait."

"What'd you do it for? Run the two guys off the road."

"Because they were asking for it, I guess."

"You could have killed them."

"I'll have to decide how to handle your friend at the hearing," Nancy said. "Should I be the sweet little girl or try to impress him?"

"I don't know," Ryan said. "I've never seen him in court. Is Ray getting you a lawyer?"

"I suppose so. We haven't discussed it."

Off the highway, on the gravel road now, the Mustang trailed a mist of dust that rose and thinned to nothing in the sun glare. On both sides of the road the fields stretched flat and empty to distant trees.

"This has all been picked," Ryan said. "They're working down a ways toward Holden now and I sure hope Bob Junior's with them." He let the Mustang crawl along, the gravel rattling against the car's underbody.

"Way over there"—Ryan pointed. "There's some pickers." He waited until they were a little farther up the road, coming even with the pickers. "See how you straddle the row? These people are the only ones who can work bent over like that all day."

"You did it," Nancy said.

"I like to broke my back. After the first day I thought I'd have to quit. I guess you have to be raised a picker to be any good. Billy Ruiz, little half-pint of a guy, he'll outpick anybody."

They moved along the ruts, Ryan squinting out at the field lying still in the August heat and at small groups of figures, far out, working slowly along the rows but appearing to be standing in one place.

"They got to get the crop in this week," Ryan said. "A few more days and they're too big for pickles and all you've got are cucumbers——"

"I love pickle facts," Nancy said.

Ryan looked at her. "Have you ever thought about it?"

"All the time."

"If the grower can't get enough pickers, I mean, good pickers to get his crop in on time, he loses his shirt. That's why he needs the migrants."

"I love farm labor facts, too."

The Mustang approached the barn and outbuildings and beyond them the row of one-story buildings that were weathered a clean gray and stood in the open like a deserted Army post left to rot. As they drew closer there were signs of life: the clothes hanging on the lines and the sound of children playing.

The children, in the worn, hard-packed field next to the barn, stood for a moment watching the Mustang, then came running after it, yelling in a mixture of English and Spanish. A woman in a T-shirt and blue jeans stood in the doorway of her home; another sat on a turned-over washtub wearing a man's straw hat. There were women in the shade of the washhouse and a woman in the open sunlight, half turned, motionless, her arms raised to the clothesline of faded denim and khaki, her gaze following the Mustang and the children running in its dust.

Ryan could hear the children and could feel the gaze of the women. He said to Nancy, "See that, like a tool shed? That's where I lived, three of us in there."

"Nice."

"I don't know. It really wasn't so bad," Ryan said. "It's true what you hear about migrant camps, the awful way the people live. But when you're living here, I mean everybody in it together, you get used to it and laugh at different things and it really isn't so bad. We'd play ball in the evening or a guy would get his guitar out and, you know, everybody would sing."

"Sounds like fun," Nancy said.

Ryan looked at her. "All right, it wasn't *fun*, but it wasn't so bad, either."

"Are you ready?" She was pouring Cold Ducks into a stem glass. She had brought the bottle in a bag of crushed ice and two glasses.

"Not right now," Ryan said.

The road curved out of the camp area and made a little jog and seemed to narrow with the trees closing in on both sides. About a hundred yards up the road they came to Ray's place. It was in a clearing with a circular drive leading in and out, a two-story farmhouse that had been faced with green-stained logs and converted into a hunting lodge.

Nancy said, "Have you been inside?"

"No, this is the closest I've been."

"He has deer heads and Indian blankets on the walls."

"Well, it's a hunting lodge," Ryan said.

He turned into the drive and followed it in low gear as he studied the place. The drive was empty and the place looked deserted; still, he kept going, following the curved drive out again to the road.

Nancy was watching him. "You didn't give it much of a look."

"I want to see if we can get up behind it," Ryan said.

He saw the sign down the road before he was able to read it. The sign was on the right, a painted board pointing across the road into the woods. Ryan wasn't looking for a sign and it didn't mean anything to him until they were close enough to read it—ROGERS—and then he remembered Mr. Majestyk telling him about the place up in the woods that would be perfect for a hunting lodge, his plan to have a couple of big A-frames stuck together with a central heating unit; that was it.

As he turned left into the dirt road Nancy said, "Now where?" She must have seen the sign, but that was all she said.

"This ought to get us up there," Ryan said.

It was a dirt road with deep ruts, narrow and winding, so narrow in places the brush and tree branches scraped the sides of the car. They moved slowly, the springs squeaking and the flat shape of the hood out in front of them rising and dipping through the chuckholes. The road began to climb, curving into switchbacks, the trees high overhead, quiet in here and dim, with patches of sunlight and glimpses of sky up through the branches. All the way up neither of them spoke, not until they were at the top and the road opened up, ending in a cleared area, and Nancy said, "Well, now that we're here."

God, it was quiet, a quiet you could feel. Ryan's door slammed loud and he stood there after he got out. Then moving and hearing only the sound of his shoes in the leaves. It was a good-sized area; it had been cleared and people had been here. He noticed a few rusted beer cans and a brown whiskey bottle and bits of paper around. Some people knew where it was, but God, it was quiet and away from everything. The only woods he had ever been in were in Detroit, in Palmer Park and on Belle Isle, and in those woods you could always hear people outside of the woods having a picnic or playing baseball. He had never been in real north-country woods.

"Now what?" Nancy said.

He didn't answer her. He walked around, over to one side of the clearing that looked down on a lake, a narrow, curved lake that sat down there by itself with thick trees growing up from its banks. He walked along the edge of the clearing, looking down into dense woods that you would have to cut your way through, to the other side, and here through an opening he could see the hunting lodge and beyond it part of the cucumber fields and the migrant camp, way down there far away, the buildings neat and orderly in the sunlight and edged with clean shadow lines. He could see the junk-heap cars back of the buildings and a little square of yellow, Luis Camacho's bus.

God, with about a hundred and twenty thousand miles on it.

"You can see the camp," Ryan said.

Nancy was still in the car, about twenty feet away. She said, "Really?"

"Come here, you can see it good. There's the bus we rode up in."

"Some other time," Nancy said.

"I don't know how that bus ever made it. It was the craziest ride I ever took. I mean, it wasn't like a bus ride, it was like living on a bus for four days." Ryan looked toward her, then walked over. "I'll have one now."

She poured Cold Duck into a glass and handed it to him. Ryan held it up, looking at the dark red color, and smiled.

"It reminds me of Billy Ruiz; he always drank rock and rye. You ever taste it? It's awful."

"Pop?"

"Terrible. It's got a reddish color." Ryan smiled again, looking at the stemmed glass. "He was always holding it up to see how much he had left. He'd be eating a lunch stick or something, take a bite, take a swallow, and then hold the bottle up and look at it, trying to make them come out even. It reminded me of that."

"Let's go," Nancy said.

Ryan had turned from the car. He was looking off into the trees, in the direction of the migrant camp.

"I don't know," he said. "The way they live and all, they always seem to get along. They don't really bitch about anything, they kid about it. I mean, I think of them as being pretty happy. I don't mean simple, fun-loving folk, you know——"

"No," Nancy said. "What *do* you mean?"

Ryan looked at her now. "I mean, they can take it. Maybe they take more than they should, I don't know. But even living the way they do, they still have something not many people have."

"I know," Nancy said. "Dignity."

"Forget it."

"How about nobility?"

Ryan finished his drink, trying to do it calmly.

"Come on, I want to know."

"Go bag your ass," Ryan said.

She smiled and started to laugh, then put her head back and laughed louder. Ryan watched her. Something was strange and he kept watching her until he realized what it was. In the three days he had known her this was the first time he had heard her laugh.

A fellow by the name of A. J. Banks, from the Growers Association, called Bob Jr. and asked him what it would cost to have the labor camp torn down and hauled away so they could plant that whole area next season. Bob Jr. said he wasn't a wrecking company, why ask him? And A. J. Banks said if he could build it, goddamnit, he could estimate tearing it down, couldn't he? Bob Jr. said he'd look it over and see what he thought. That's why he drove up to the camp and would have sworn he saw Nancy's Mustang heading out the back road as he reached the migrant buildings. Maybe not.

But maybe it was her car. After he looked over the buildings and got an idea how many truckloads it would take to haul the lumber away, he drove out the back road. Her car wasn't at Mr. Ritchie's lodge. Beyond the lodge the road didn't lead anywhere; it cut through pastureland and woods and finally reached the lakeshore about fifteen miles from Geneva Beach. Bob Jr. hadn't been back here since spring, since they decided to sell the woods property and he put the sign up on the road. Once in a while somebody, like Mr. Majestyk, would look at the property, but usually the only ones who came by were kids looking for a place to make out. The tire tracks could be anybody's; old ones. But then he remembered it had rained the day before yesterday.

When he saw the good clean impression of the tracks turning into their private road, he knew somebody had been back here recently. He wasn't thinking of Nancy now. He'd decided it couldn't have been her car he'd seen. But he was curious about the tire tracks. That's why he shifted into first and headed the pickup truck up the private road.

The first thing Ryan did when he saw the pickup, hearing it first and knowing it right away as it came out of the trees, he placed his glass on the hood of the Mustang and looked around. He wasn't trying to be casual about it, but he wasn't hurrying either. He spotted a tree limb on the ground, over just a little way, and by the time Bob Jr. was out of the pickup, Ryan had snapped off a branch the size of a broom handle and stood resting on it in his spearman pose.

In the car, holding her glass, her arm resting on the doorsill, Nancy said, "Hi, Bob," and waited to see what would happen.

Bob Jr. looked over the situation. He saw Nancy and the empty glass on the hood and out beyond the car Jack Ryan holding his staff or club or whatever the hell it was. They were both waiting for him to do something, like it was up to him to make the next move. Ryan was standing there asking for it and that part of it was simple: he'd told Ryan to leave and Ryan was still here, so he'd have to teach him a lesson. But with Nancy watching, he'd have to make it look easy, like this bird wasn't any trouble at all. Bob Jr. took off his cowboy hat and his sunglasses and put them in the truck, through the window.

"Bob," Nancy said, "do you want a Cold Duck?"

"Not just now," Bob Jr. said. He glanced at her. "What're you doing out here?" As he said it, it didn't sound right to him.

"I don't know," Nancy said. "He brought me."

"Has he bothered you any?"

"Let's see—no, he hasn't really *bothered* me." She was having fun.

"A ball bat or a stick," Bob Jr. said, staring at Ryan again. "You got to have something in your hand, don't you?"

Ryan didn't answer. He stood waiting.

"Tough guy if he's got a club in his hand. Hey, boy, don't you want to fight fair?"

Ryan frowned now. He said, "Fair? What is this, the goddamn Golden Gloves?"

"A man fights with his fists," Bob Jr. said.

"Yeah, well you come at me, buddy, and I'll hit you with the heaviest thing I can find."

"I got a tire iron in the truck," Bob Jr. said. "Maybe I better get it."

"If you did," Ryan said then, "and we started swinging at each other, tell me something, what would we be fighting about?"

"Because you think you're a tough boy and think you can take me."

"Did I ever tell you that?"

"You didn't have to. I know your smart-ass type the minute I see it."

Ryan kept studying him. "You really want to fight, uh?"

"You got something coming," Bob Jr. said.

Ryan looked at Nancy then and said, "Tell him he doesn't have to."

She was watching Ryan. "It's not up to me."

155

"Tell him anyway."

"Leave her out of it," Bob Jr. said.

Ryan shook his head. "Boy, you must be awful dumb or something. She wants a fight, don't you see that?"

"And you want to get out of it," Bob Jr. said.

It was coming now and Ryan knew it. Every time he had ever been in a fight since he was little, he knew this time when his stomach tightened and he could see in the other guy's eyes they were going to go through with it. He had thought about it a lot, this moment, and he had come to realize that the other guy must be feeling and thinking the same thing, and no matter how big the other guy was, he would probably be afraid or tightened up or nervous, because nobody could ever be a hundred percent sure. This moment, Ryan had decided, when they weren't quite ready, was the time to hit them. Hit first and hit hard and maybe end it right there.

Bob Jr. made it easier. He took a couple of steps back just as Ryan was ready to move and half turned to reach into the pickup bed. He had to look in to locate the tire iron or a wrecking bar and as he glanced around again to check on Ryan he would never have thought a man could move so fast; Ryan was rushing him, steps away, and the goddamn staff or club or whatever it was, up in the air, was coming down on him.

Bob Jr. rolled against the side of the pickup box, getting his head behind a shoulder, and took the first blow hard and solid against his forearm as he brought it up.

His arm felt numb and he must have closed his eyes. He didn't see the club come at him again, he was guarding his head, and the goddamn thing whacked solid against his left knee. There was nothing to do then but rush the son of a bitch and he took another good one, stinging across his left shoulder, before he got in close and got both hands on the heavy tree branch and felt it hard and round and the bark coarse in his hands, straining against it to take it away from Ryan and then seeing Ryan's face right in front of his, the face tight and straining, looking right into his eyes.

"You're through now, boy," Bob Jr. said, and barely

156

finished saying it as Ryan's left fist came off the tree branch and jabbed straight into his face.

For Ryan it was right now—as Bob Jr. went back and his face was raised and open—take it right now quick was all he could think of, now while he was pressing and had him, and he jabbed his left straight into the face again, staying with the guy as he went back, jabbing with the left and jabbing a right to the face, setting it up and now, right now, coming in with the long left hand from behind his shoulder, hitting solid, feeling it all the way up his arm and seeing the guy stumble back with blood coming out of his nose, but God—and it was an awful feeling, the worst feeling you can have—the guy didn't go down.

He let go of the tree branch and stood there, his face bloody, looking at Ryan, breathing, getting his breath, wiping his hand across his mouth. Ryan brought up his guard as Bob Jr. came at him, his arms already heavy and tired.

Nancy took time to pour herself a little Cold Duck and she sipped it while she watched them hit each other. Bob Jr. was bigger, in fact Jackie looked sort of frail next to him, but he had drawn blood first and Bob Jr. was a mess, blood all over his mouth and down the front of his checkered shirt. He didn't seem to care, though. She watched him move in, taking Ryan's jabs on his shoulder, then another good one—wow—right in the mouth, but this time he didn't stop, he came in swinging that big right fist and slammed it into Ryan's face. It must have stunned him; he hesitated and Bob hit him again and again until Ryan dropped to his knees.

That's it, Nancy thought. Pretty good while it lasted. She was surprised when Ryan came up, very slowly at first; then, before Bob Jr. knew it, Ryan was swinging at him. He got him hard in the face and for a moment they stood close, both swinging at each other with everything they had. Until Ryan dropped.

He went to his hands and knees, his head down, and this time he didn't try to get up. God, his hands hurt, and his mouth. He wanted to touch his mouth and his jaw, but he was afraid if he raised either hand from the ground, he'd fall on his face. The guy could stand there if he wanted; Ryan decided he wasn't getting up anymore.

But the guy wasn't standing there. Ryan turned his head to the side and the guy was sitting down just a few feet away with his head back, looking up at the sky with his eyes closed and pressing a handkerchief to his nose.

Ryan rolled over to a sitting position. God, his shoulders hurt too. He sat there looking at the guy and finally he said, "That's not the way to do it."

Bob Jr. opened his eyes and looked over at Ryan.

"That doesn't stop it," Ryan said.

"Yeah," Bob Jr. said in his handkerchief. "You put your head back."

"That's a lot of crap," Ryan said. "You blow your nose and then hold it, pinch it, with your head forward."

"You're crazy."

"Everybody thinks you put your head back," Ryan said, "but you don't, you put it forward. Go on."

Bob Jr. leaned forward and the blood dripped out on the ground as he took his handkerchief away.

"Go on, blow it," Ryan said. He watched him to see if he did it right.

After about a minute Bob Jr. said, "I never seen so much blood since I dressed a buck I shot right here last fall." His voice was nasal and muffled in the handkerchief.

"There's a lot of deer in the woods here?"

"A lot? You go look at the game trails going down to that lake where they water."

"I never been hunting."

"This buck I got, I walked up from the road and he was standing here waiting."

"What'd you use?"

"I use different guns. That time I had me an old O-three, I mean old, but the son of a bitch'd shoot from here to Holden."

"This guy Walter Majestyk," Ryan said, "he was talking about a lodge up here."

"You know him?"

"I work for him."

"Hey," Nancy said. She was still in the car. "Is this the intermission or what?"

Ryan looked at Bob Jr. "I'm going to get in that car and drive out of here. You got any objections?"

Bob Jr. said, "What do I care what you do?"

He was still sitting there when they left.

Neither of them spoke until they were down out of the woods and moving along the back road to the migrant camp. He could feel her watching him and finally he said, "You got what you wanted, didn't you?"

"That wasn't very nice, trying to blame me." Nancy sat against her door, watching him. "How do you feel?"

"Like I've been hit in the face."

"You don't look so bad. Here." She handed him her glass and watched him finish it, holding the wine in his mouth and letting it burn before swallowing it. His teeth felt sore and loose in his jaw; when he worked it, he could hear a clicking sound close to his ear. His hands hurt and they looked awful from hitting the guy in the face after he'd started bleeding. Nancy took the glass from him and he held the steering wheel low with one hand. Up ahead he saw a group of pickers coming out of the field, several of them walking along the side of the road and looking back as they heard the car coming.

"It settles one thing," Ryan said.

"What?"

"I'm not going in that hunting lodge. I don't care how much is in there."

Nancy stared straight ahead through the windshield; she was in no hurry. Looking at Ryan finally, she said, "I knew you were going to say that. I didn't know when or how you'd say it, but I knew you would."

"Well, you're smarter than I am," Ryan said, "because I just found out."

"No, you didn't. You might have thought you were going to rob the place," Nancy said, "but you never would. I thought you might change, but you haven't. You're a small-time breaking and entering man, Jackie. That's all you are. You can dream about taking fifty thousand, but you'd never do it."

"Look," Ryan said, "he saw us up there. The police say to him, 'Did you see anybody around the place the last few days?' And right away he remembers us. He remembers *me* and he starts to put things together."

"You're a little upset," Nancy said.

"You bet I am."

"You're mad because you think I provoked the fight."

"That's something else," Ryan said.

"But the point is, Bob seeing us doesn't prove anything."

"I'm not going to give it a chance to," Ryan said.

"We'll talk about it later, after I've cleaned you up. How does that sound?"

"I don't see there's anything to talk about."

They were coming up on the pickers now, who were edging back from the shoulder of the road to let the car pass. As they approached them Ryan said, "Put the glass on the floor."

Frank Pizarro came into the light of the shed doorway after the car had passed and stood looking at the dust hanging in the air. Billy Ruiz was on the other side of the road; he had come out of the field, crossed the ditch and stood at the edge of the road gazing after the car; now he crossed over to the shed.

"That looked like Jack," he said.

"Sure it was," Pizarro said. "Showing us his car and his little chickie."

"I wave to him," Billy Ruiz said, "but he was already by me."

"He saw you."

"I don't think so."

"He saw you," Pizarro said. "He saw all of us."

"Then, why didn't he wave?"

"He's Mr. Jack Ryan in the car now."

Billy Ruiz shook his head. "No, he didn't see us. He would have waved."

"Christ, shut up with the waving! He don't care about you. He don't see you anymore."

Pizarro turned from the doorway into the darkness of the shed. He found a cigarette and lit it and then went down on his blanket to get away from Billy Ruiz and the rest of them so he could think about Ryan and the girl with no clothes on and get something straight in his mind.

All right, he had sold the beer case of wallets to the girl. Last night was something he couldn't stop thinking about: the girl coming out of the swimming pool and drying herself in front of him, not trying to hide herself, while they discussed Jack Ryan and the wallets. She put on the blouse and the shorts and he told her again, five hundred, that was the price. Then the girl going in the house and coming out with eighty dollars, with her blouse still unbuttoned. He should have kept the beer case until she got more money, but there was the eighty; it wasn't any five hundred, but she was offering it to him.

He should have sold her the wallets one at a time. Go back once a week and she would have to pay him without any clothes on.

He should have taken her in the house or put her down on the grass. She had been asking for it and it would be something to do it to her, Mr. Ritchie's girl; but because she was Mr. Ritchie's girl, he had not touched her, because he couldn't believe it—the not having any clothes on—and because he had been afraid if he touched her, something would happen. He didn't know what. Something.

All right, he should have done a lot of things it was too late to do. But he still had one thing left, if he could get it straight in his mind how to say it to her and make her believe it. He still knew about Ryan and he could still call the police and tell them it was Ryan that robbed the place Sunday.

So the idea was to go to her at night when Ryan wasn't there and tell her how much it would cost for him not to call the police, sticking to the five hundred this time and not coming down to any lousy eighty bucks.

He began to put words together, the way he would say it to her. Like: "If you don't have the money, have your boyfriend steal you some. I don't care where you get it."

The important words: "Get me five hundred or I call the police."

But as he lay on his blanket smoking the cigarette, in

161

this dim oven of a place with its tin-shed roof and smell of mold, Frank Pizarro said to himself, Wait. What are you talking about the police for? Why the police. Man, you see it? There's somebody better than the police.

Tell her, she don't pay, you write a letter to Mr. Ritchie.

THIRTEEN

AT FIRST, OPENING HIS EYES AND MOVING, feeling the soreness in his shoulders, Ryan didn't know where he was. Settling again, stretching his legs and moving his hands over the cool aluminum arms of the lounge chair, he had a good feeling from the soreness, a feeling of having worked and finished something. He was glad he had fought the guy and it was over. He was glad the guy had seen them.

Maybe he was never going in at all and it had been just talk. Maybe if Bob Jr. hadn't showed up, he would have thought of some other excuse. Or maybe when the time came he would have taken off. He wasn't sure.

Or maybe he was just tired. No, that wasn't it. He was tired all right, and sore; but that didn't have anything to do with it. It was something else.

It was a feeling of relief. He could come right out and say to himself, You don't have to break into the place. You don't have to take the money and go through all that. You don't have to get involved and worry about her bragging about it to somebody. You don't have to be waiting for something to happen. You don't have to even think about it anymore.

He felt like a cigarette. He touched his shirt pocket; it was flat. He couldn't see if there were cigarettes on the umbrella table; it was too dark over there. Turning to look at the table, he turned a little more to look at the house. The room off the patio was dark, though a faint light was coming from somewhere in the back part of the room. The upstairs windows were dark. He wondered if she had gone to bed. He didn't know what time it was. After ten anyway. He must have slept about three hours. He thought about going for a swim to loosen up but decided it would be too much trouble and it wouldn't help much. Tomorrow when he woke up, he'd be so stiff and sore it would hurt to move and there wasn't anything he could do about it. He wondered why she hadn't left a light on.

Nancy heard him on the outside stairs and now, sitting in the oversized chair in the dark, she saw him on the sun deck; she watched him slide open the glass door and come in; she watched him pause, getting his bearings, then start for the den. When he was within a few feet of her chair, Nancy said, "Hi."

He didn't answer right away. She had surprised him and it took a few seconds for him to locate her and think of something to say.

"I was going to surprise you," Ryan said.

"I don't sleep in the den." Nancy waited.

Ryan leaned close to her chair to turn on the lamp.

"Where do you sleep?"

"Upstairs."

"Show me."

"After," Nancy said. "I brought up everything we'll need."

"Like what?"

"From the bar." Nancy watched him, her head slightly lowered, her eyes raised. Ryan stared back at her. It was her half-assed Ann-Margaret look, but it was all right.

"The beer's in the fridge," Nancy said. She didn't move.

"I don't think I feel like anything."

"I do," Nancy said.

"I didn't think you drank beer."

"Sometimes. Will you get me one?" She watched him go to the kitchen and in the corner of her eye saw him

163

reach in and turn on the light. She heard the refrigerator door open and, after a moment, close.

From the kitchen he said, "There isn't any beer."

Nancy stared at the sliding glass door, at the darkness outside, and the dim reflection of the room. She could see herself sitting in the chair. "Look in the cupboard next to the fridge. Bottom shelf."

"What're you English, you like warm beer?"

"Put a couple of bottles in the freezer. It'll only take a few minutes."

"Maybe we should have something else."

"I don't want something else, I want beer."

Ryan looked in. "I believe you."

She waited. She heard him open the cupboard. There were faint sounds. Then silence. She counted a thousand and one, a thousand and two, a thousand and three a thousand and four—

"You don't have any beer," Ryan said.

She looked over her shoulder, past the corner of the backrest, to Ryan in the doorway.

"You've got a bunch of old wallets, but you don't have any beer."

Nancy twisted around, leaning on the chair arm. "Do you recognize them?"

He stared back at her. He stared thoughtfully, taking his time. Finally he came into the living room. He drew up the ottoman of Nancy's chair and sat down.

"I have never been mean to a girl," Ryan said. "I have never talked loud to a girl or ever hit a girl."

"There's beer downstairs," Nancy said.

"Maybe I'll have something else."

"Help yourself. Behind the bar. The beer's in the fridge underneath."

"Do you always say that?"

"What?"

"Fridge."

She frowned a little. "Not always."

"It's a dumb word," Ryan said. He got up and went down the circular stairs to the activities room. A lamp at one end of the bar spread a soft pink light over the polished wood. He found a bottle of bourbon and poured some of it into an Old Fashioned glass. He took ice and beer from the refrigerator, put two cubes into the glass, and opened the beer. He lit a cigarette from a dish of filter-tipped cigarettes on the bar; he blew the smoke out slowly and took a sip of the bourbon.

Nancy had not moved. She waited as Ryan placed the beer and a glass and the bottle of bourbon on the table next to her and sat down on the ottoman.

"All right," Ryan said. "Tell me the name of the game." He watched her patiently.

"You sound different," Nancy said, "at different times. I'll bet you're moody."

"Tell me the game, okay?"

"Being moody is all right if you have something to be moody about, but I think most people pretend, like a pose."

Ryan drank the rest of his bourbon and stood up. "I'll see you."

"The game," Nancy said, "is called unless you're a nice boy and do what I tell you, I'll go to the state police with the wallets. It's sort of a long name for a game, but it's fun."

"It is a long name," Ryan said. "Why do you think I have anything to do with them?"

"Because your friend told me. Frank something. He came here last night and said he'd go to the police unless I gave him five hundred dollars for the wallets."

"Five hundred?"

"He settled for eighty."

"Why did he think you'd be interested?"

"I guess because he saw you with my car. He decided we must have a thing going."

"Well," Ryan said, "that's his story."

"No, it's my story now," Nancy said. "I'll say I saw you come out of the house. I followed you and picked up the case when you threw it away."

"You're going to a lot of trouble."

"Because I need you."

Ryan shook his head. "No, I think you've got the wrong guy."

"And I think if your friend was arrested," Nancy said, "he'd blame the whole thing on you."

Ryan sat down again. He poured bourbon over the melting ice cubes and sipped it, seeing Frank Pizaro in a straight chair with the sheriff's cop, J. R. Coleman, standing over him.

"I think you might have something," Ryan said.

"Good."

"Yes, I can see that."

Nancy smiled. "Very good. I thought you might be mad at first, but you're taking it like a little man."

"I want to get it straight," Ryan said. "If I back out of our deal, you'll call the police and put them on Frank Pizarro."

"Right."

"You don't care about Bob Junior seeing us."

"Not at all."

"I'll have to think about it," Ryan said. He raised his glass. "Can I get some more ice?"

"Help yourself."

"I don't guess you want another beer."

"I hate beer."

He got ice from the refrigerator in the kitchen and came out carrying the beer case. Nancy watched him drop it on the ottoman.

"I've thought it over," Ryan said. "No."

Nancy waited a moment. "Okay."

"So I better take this with me."

"Go ahead. I don't need it."

He sat on the edge of the ottoman, facing her, his knees touching her legs tucked under her. "Look," he said, "don't do anything dumb, all right? People start telling on each other it gets to be a mess. The police start asking you questions and it gets in the newspaper and whether you like it or not, everybody knows your business. You don't want that, do you? I mean you got a good deal here, what do you want to wreck it for?"

"I was just thinking," Nancy said, "your little job Sunday will be in the Geneva paper tomorrow. They'll be talking about it in town."

"For a couple of days maybe."

"Everybody will keep their doors locked."

"That's another thing," Ryan said. "Bob Junior will read about a robbery and have it on his mind. I mean, our timing is bad."

"Why don't you relax?" Nancy said. She took his cigarette and drew on it before settling back in the chair. She gave Ryan her nice smile and a soft, warm look with her eyes.

"I was just playing," she said then. "Do you really think I'd go to the police?"

"If you thought it might be fun."

"Jackie—" Sounding hurt, disappointed.

"And if you thought you could stay out of it," Ryan said. "But that's what I mean. You can't stay out of it. They put your picture in the paper and your life story and everybody knows your business. It puts Ray on the spot and he dumps you, like that."

Nancy pressed close to one arm of the chair, making room and patting the seat cushion. "Come on over," she said, and gave him her sympathetic pout look. "Come on, let's be friends."

He had the feeling he shouldn't move too fast—like reaching out to pet an animal that might take his hand off if he didn't do it gently. All the wallets were in the beer case with all the names in the wallets of the people who had been robbed and a minute before she had been holding the case over him, ready to drop it on him. Now she was a girl sitting there, being a girl, trying to hook him the old way and pretty sure she could do it. And even turning on the fake girl stuff, she looked better than any girl he had ever seen before.

What Ryan did, sliding in beside her, he put his hands against the back of the chair and moved in to get his mouth on hers, his hands supporting him before sliding down to her shoulders, her hands coming up around his neck and fooling with his hair as she pressed against him. Their mouths came slightly apart, giving her just enough room to say, "Let's go upstairs."

He walked home carrying the beer case, along the beach, along the cold-sand edge of the water, feeling the

167

night breeze and the soreness in his jaw and shoulders. He saw himself walking along the beach in the darkness, then saw himself standing by the bed buttoning his shirt and pushing it down into his pants, Nancy a soft, dark shape against the white sheets, lying on her back unmoving, one hand on her stomach, her legs a little apart, her eyes looking at him with a calm, nothing look. He had dressed in front of girls lying in bed before. He had said things that made them laugh or giggle or smile; he had grabbed for them again and wrestled with them and rolled off the bed with them and had slapped their bare tails and said, "See you," and some of them he had seen again and some he hadn't. He liked girls. He had never forced a girl to go to bed if she didn't want to. He had never said, "Come on, if you really love me." He had had fun with girls and the girls had had fun. He thought he had had fun with Nancy. Now he wasn't sure. Did he have fun with her because he was with her or did he have fun only because he'd gone through the motions and only the motions were fun?

Every one of the other girls he could remember had been a living person and now he wondered if he had ever thought of Nancy as a person. He couldn't picture her when she was alone. He couldn't picture her yawning with no one watching. The broad in the back seat of the station wagon, the ten-buck broad with the two guys and the dollar-a-bottle beer—he didn't picture her as a person, either. Thinking about it didn't make sense and he became aware of himself again, the sand and the darkness and the surf coming in. He put the beer case down and cupped his hands against the breeze to light a cigarette. He saw his hands in the glow of the match. He saw himself walking along again: a hot dog Jack Ryan who had just notched up another one and was now having his smoke.

And Leon Woody says—

No, Leo doesn't say anything. Jack Ryan says it. He says the hot dog only thinks he notched one up, like any hot dog who thinks he's a hot dog. But what happened, *he* was notched. Hooked, notched, and set up.

Whatever he did now, he had to do something with the

beer case first. He was approaching the Bay Vista and he thought of the vacant field next to Mr. Majestyk's house.

Ryan was exactly the way Nancy imagined he would be. Very basic but in control, and thorough. Sort of a natural. Neat body—bone and muscle and good moves—which he had probably been working on since he'd first discovered there were girls in the world. He had to pose after, taking his time getting dressed, and she had pictured him doing that too.

Jackie was all right. It would be fun to grab the money and meet him in Detroit and spend about a week with him in Florida or on Grand Bahama and then, before breaking it off, take him home to meet Mother.

Lying on the bed, one hand on her stomach, her other hand playing with a strand of her hair, Nancy heard herself say, "Mother, this is Jack Ryan." She saw her mother in the shade of the palm tree, her cigarette case, lighter, and vodka and tonic on the glass-top table. She saw her mother lower the thick novel to her lap, slip off her reading glasses, and hold them, interrupted, under her chin, her eyes on Ryan and her mouth forming the smallest gesture of a smile. Her head would be cocked very slightly, alertly, and she would seem to nod, a slight smile and a pleasant hint of a nod, but not giving away any of herself in the look: withdrawn, peering at him through little brown stones, observing him and sensing something was wrong.

"Jack's from Detroit, Mother."

Watch the eyes, the little brown stones. Watch Jack Ryan. He looks away from Mother. Mother isn't bad-looking at all for a forty-four-year-old mother, chic and slick and wearing white and pearls to set off her tan. But Ryan isn't sure about her. She hasn't said anything, but she scares him. Little Mother pushes him off-balance with her cool. He looks around the patio. He puts one hand in his pocket to show he's at ease and looks at the small, curved swimming pool and then toward the white stucco house, trying to think of something to say. It would be good, Nancy thought. It would be fun to bring him in and let him loose. It would be fun to watch mother watching him: afraid he might touch something or come toward her, watching him calmly but afraid to move, sitting perfectly still and waiting for him to go away.

"Mother, this is Jack Ryan. He breaks into houses and almost clubbed a man to death." That could shake her up a little.

Maybe. Though the thing with the two boys in Lauderdale didn't seem to shake her—the two boys she had met at Bahia Mar and had brought home because her mother was out and only Loretta, the maid, would be there.

She was fifteen then. She could still see the two boys standing with their hands on their hips in shorts and tight football jerseys with numerals, 23 and 30-something. They were both over six feet and could chugalug a can of beer in less than twenty seconds, tall and slouchy with their hands-on-hips, time-out pose, but still little boys. She didn't put them in the same class now with Jack Ryan. Size didn't count. Anyone under 21 or who wasn't married (a new qualification) or had never been arrested for felonious assault, was still a minor.

They sat by the little curved pool with three six-packs and a transistor radio and the boys beat time on the arms of their chairs when they weren't drinking the beer. Loretta, black face and white uniform, would appear at the door leading into the sunroom, frowning and trying to catch Nancy's eye. One of the boys said, "Your maid wants you." But Nancy pretended she didn't see Loretta and the two boys got the idea.

Nancy said, "It's too bad we have to be spied on. If we were alone, we'd probably have more fun." One of the boys said, "Yeah," and the other one said, "Like doing what?" And Nancy said, "Like going swimming." One of them said, "But we didn't bring any suits." And Nancy said, "So?"

She watched them each drink their beer while they thought of a way to get rid of Loretta and while Nancy knew all the time how they would do it. They couldn't lock her in her room; Loretta had the key.

So they used the box spring and mattress from Nancy's room, sliding them quietly over the tile to Loretta's open door. She didn't see them. When she did look up, and they heard her muffled voice inside, a wall of striped mattress ticking covered the doorway. They laughed, Nancy laughed with them leaning against the box spring while they brought chairs to wedge between the mattress and the opposite wall in the hallway. Then they ran outside and took off their clothes and dove in. The boys did. Nancy went to her room and put on a two-piece semibikini. She turned off all the lights in the house and the swimming pool lights too, hearing the boys yelling hey, what's going on! But when she came out and they saw her, they grinned and one of them whistled and the other one said, "Hey, now, *yes!*" The wet young athletes in their wet, sagging jockey shorts.

They played tag, with a lot of running dives and grabbing under water, stopping for a swig of beer every few minutes. After enough of that Nancy fell into a lounge chair to rest, her chest rising and her flat stomach sucking in as she breathed. They sat staring at her until she got up and stretched, showing them her stomach again, and said she was going in to change.

Hey, but would one of them mind unhooking her bra? It was so darn hard to reach.

They both went for it, and while they pushed and wrestled for position, Nancy reached behind and unfastened the strap. Walking to the sunroom door, she knew they were watching. She went inside, closed the glass door behind her, and pressed the lock catch. She took off the bra. She stood with her back to the glass until she knew they were close to the door and one of them was trying the handle. Then she turned around.

One of them said, "Hey, come on. Open the door."

Nancy looked from one to the other, the tall stringy athletes trying to look casual in their wet jockey shorts. She hooked her thumbs in the low waist of the bikini and smiled.

"Come on. Open up."

"What'll you give me?" Nancy asked them.

"You know what." They both laughed at that.

"Come on," the other one said again.

"I'm going to bed," Nancy said.

"Open the door, we'll go with you."

"What'll you give me?" Nancy said again.

They were both looking at her, seriously now, silent. Finally one of them said, "What do you want, anyway?"

And Nancy said, "Fifty bucks, Charlie. Each."

She could still see the dumb look on their faces.

And the look on her mother's face a few days later, the no-look look.

"Is it true, Nancy?"

Her mother had found out about the two boys because one of them happened to have a buddy relationship with his father. The little buddy told the big buddy. The big buddy told his wife, who told a friend, who told Nancy's mother, the friend saying she didn't believe a word of it, but perhaps Nancy's mother would like to look into it. Then the scene—her mother sitting in the living room, Loretta a few steps behind her.

"Is it true, Nancy?"

The brown stones in her mother's solemn eyes stared up at her and, watching her mother's eyes very closely, she said, "Yes, it's true."

The eyes did not seem to change expression. "Do you know what you're saying?" her mother asked. "You want us to believe you offered yourself to those boys?"

"Uh-huh."

"Don't say uh-huh, dear. Say yes or no."

"Yes."

"All right, tell me why."

"I don't know."

"If you think this is cute—have you thought of the consequences?"

Nancy hesitated, interested. "What consequences?"

"That people," her mother said quietly, "might hear about it?"

Nancy began to smile; she couldn't help it. "Mother, you're beautiful."

"I don't see anything amusing," her mother said. "I want to know what happened."

Nancy looked at Loretta, who looked at Nancy's mother. "Whatever you heard is probably true."

"Loretta said they left before midnight."

"How long do you think it takes?" Nancy said.

Her mother's solemn expression held. "I want you to admit you thought this up as a not very funny joke."

"Mother, I did. I propositioned them."

"All right," her mother said, rising, smoothing her dress over her hips. "There doesn't seem to be much point in talking about it."

"Really. It's true."

"It's up to you," her mother said. "But until you admit the truth and start making sense, you won't be allowed out of the house." Her mother turned and started across the room.

"I'll tell you everything we did," Nancy said after her. "Do you want to hear it or not?"

Her mother didn't. A few days later she told her mother only part of the story was true, the part about blocking Loretta's door. Her mother said, then the boys made up the rest of it as some sort of perverted joke. Yes, Nancy said, and she was allowed to go outside again and play.

It had been all right but very minor. She had been a little girl then and now she was a big girl and had to think as a big girl. Everything was relative. It became relative as one changed one's approach and went on to bigger and better bounces.

Playing with the two boys had been fun.

Faking out the fathers taking her home from babysitting had been fun.

Putting on Bob Jr. had been fun.

Fooling around with Jack Ryan and thinking of how to take Ray's fifty thousand had been fun. But even this was fairly low key compared to what she had in mind now.

If she could set it up. If she could work out the timing, it would be the biggest bounce of all.

FOURTEEN

RYAN SKIMMED OUT THE SWIMMING POOL,
with the little Fisher kids watching and asking him if they
could jump in and try and touch the end of the skimmer,
but he told them he had to hurry and didn't have time to
fool around. He didn't feel like playing. He got the rake
and cardboard box without running into Mr. Majestyk
and took them down to the beach. There was no one
down there yet and it was a good place to think.

First, was there anything to worry about or not?

There was always something to worry about when
other people were involved.

Even before Nancy presented him with the beer case,
there was something to worry about. He had gotten rid of
the beer case. He had taken care of that early this morning, burying it five feet deep in the vacant lot. But he
hadn't gotten rid of Nancy. He hadn't gotten rid of Billy
Ruiz or Frank Pizarro. They were all hanging over him
and could fall on him and maybe the only way was to run
out from under. Disappear.

He could still go into Ray's lodge. It would still be pos-
sible to pull it off.

It was a funny thing, he could see himself going into
the place, but he didn't look right. He could see himself
going into other places with Nancy, the great boy-girl
burglary team, and that didn't look right, either. He
looked dumb, doing it because she wanted to do it. A
game and not real at all. She talked about real life. It
wouldn't be anything like real life. It wouldn't be anything like going into places with Leon Woody. That had
been real. But now it seemed like a long time ago and
something that would never happen again. Like hanging

from the roof. He did it and still had it to take out and look at, but he knew he would never hang from a roof again.

He felt some sand inside his right sneaker. He had the shoe off and was pouring the sand out when he saw Mr. Majestyk coming across the beach. He hadn't seen Mr. Majestyk since Wednesday night, after they had looked in his window. Ryan thought of it now, but he said to himself, the hell with him, and looked right at Mr. Majestyk.

Mr. Majestyk's gaze shifted beyond Ryan and moved around the beach, squinting a little in the sunlight. He said, "What're you doing?"

"What am I doing? I'm raking the beach."

Mr. Majestyk was staring at Ryan now, for a moment frowning. "What happened to you?"

"Nothing."

"I can see nothing."

"This guy and I had a disagreement."

"Boy, you get in an argument you start swinging, don't you?"

"I didn't start it."

"Listen, there's some painting has to be done in number five. I painted most of it in the spring, but I didn't get the kitchen."

"What about the beach?" Ryan looked off in the direction Nancy would come.

"Leave it," Mr. Majestyk said.

"They'll be coming down pretty soon."

"That's all right. It's not bad."

"I don't know," Ryan said. "There's some junk over there and up by the steps."

"All right, just get that. Then I'll give you the paint. Just in the kitchen where the goddamn wall's messed up. Number Five."

Ryan looked at him, realizing Mr. Majestyk had said it before. "Five? The broad by herself?"

"Yeah, she checked out yesterday, so it's a good chance before the new people come tomorrow."

"Number Five?"

"I said Five, didn't I?"

"What time did she leave?"

"In the afternoon."

"What for? What'd she say?"

"How do I know what for. She says she's leaving, she leaves. I don't ask her why. I say hope you enjoyed yourself and come back. That's all. Look, pick up that crap and then come by, I'll give you the paint." He started to walk off, then turned to Ryan again. "What were you making all the goddamn noise about this morning?"

"What noise?"

"With the bulldozer. Christ, seven thirty in the morning."

"I wanted to finish it up. I figured there'd be a lot to do today."

"Christ, seven thirty. I was about to come out, you stopped."

"Well, it's done now," Ryan said.

He dragged out raking the beach another half hour, until Mr. Majestyk appeared again and yelled to him to knock off for lunch. Looking up the beach he still saw no sign of her. So quit worrying, he thought. If she wanted him, she'd have to find him.

They had tunafish salad and onions, tomatoes and peppers and some sweet corn and the homemade bread, and a couple of beers each. They discussed whether beer was better in bottles or cans, and then which was better, bottled or draft, and both agreed, finally, that it didn't make a hell of a lot of difference. Long as it was cold.

Mr. Majestyk said hey, the game was on TV tonight. Detroit at Boston. McLain going against McDermott.

"About eight or eight thirty I think it starts."

"I'll see." Ryan said.

He wouldn't take a job as a painter for anything, though he didn't mind it once in a while. It was something different and it was quiet in here.

Ryan finished a cupboard door and got down off the chair. He could see the broad's face close to his. He lit a cigarette and went into the bedroom. Putting the cigarette in his mouth, he unlocked the window and pulled up on it. He pressed in closer and pushed up against the frame

176

with the heels of his hands. He banged them against the frame and pushed up again. The window wouldn't budge. He could see where the dried paint held the frame to the sill. The window probably hadn't been opened since spring.

He could see her face again, close, her eyes open wide inches from his. To the great lover it had been a look of wild-eyed passion. Now, in the empty room, he knew it had been pure panic. The poor broad had wanted her window opened and he had almost raped her.

He wished he could run into her again, just for a minute. He'd tell her: "Listen, I'm sorry we had that misunderstanding. See I thought—" Maybe not that; something like it. He'd have to say something.

No he wouldn't. He'd never see her again.

But he saw her in his mind every once in a while as he painted and each time he saw her, he slapped the paint on a little heavier.

She should have stayed another day. He could have been nice to her. Polite. He could have taken her out and bought her a Tom Collins and it would have been the biggest thing that ever happened to her.

The other day he could have treated Billy Ruiz a little better.

He began thinking about Billy Ruiz and the others, wondering how they were going to get home if they couldn't pay Camacho for the bus ride.

If it was true about the bus—Camacho wanting to charge them five hundred dollars.

And Pizarro wanting five hundred for the wallets. What was this, everything costing five hundred dollars? If he did anything, he should go out and have a talk with Frank about the wallets and find out about the bus.

Mr. Majestyk came in looking up at the freshly painted light green walls.

"Inside the cupboards, too," he said.

"Inside? Who's going to see inside?"

"You got enough paint?"

"I guess so."

"There's a phone call for you," Mr. Majestyk said.

177

"Yeah? Who is it?"

"Who do you think?"

He followed Mr. Majestyk to his house, wiping his hands with a rag soaked in thinner. In the living room he put the rag in his back pocket and picked up the phone with the tips of his fingers. Mr. Majestyk went over to his desk and opened and closed drawers, then shuffled through a stack of third-class mail.

"Hello?"

"Hi. I slept in this morning," Nancy said. "After the workout."

"I wondered," Ryan said. "I didn't see you."

"Are you coming over tonight?"

"I guess I could."

"Nine thirty," Nancy said.

"That late, uh?"

"I've got a surprise for you."

"No, you haven't," Ryan said. "Not anymore."

"Really. But you have to come on time."

"Okay, then."

"Will you come?"

"Yeah, okay."

"Is someone there?"

"Uh-huh."

"The one who answered?"

"Right."

"I think he was mad he had to look for you. I told him it was urgent."

"Uh-huh."

"He'll think I have hot pants."

"Okay then, I'll see you later."

"Nine thirty," Nancy said. "Come upstairs. I'll leave the door open. Okay?"

"Okay," Ryan said.

She hung up.

As Ryan put the receiver down Mr. Majestyk straightened up from the desk. "While you're here," he said, "Maybe you better take some more paint."

"I got enough."

"Just in case."

"I got plenty."

178

"Listen," Mr. Majestyk said then. "That broad on the phone——"

"Yeah?"

Mr. Majestyk smiled, self-conscious, showing his white perfect teeth. He shrugged then. "Why should I say anything—right? You're old enough."

"I was about to mention it," Ryan said. He started out but stopped in the doorway and looked back at Mr. Majestyk. "What was that broad's name in Number Five?"

After work he asked Mr. Majestyk if he could borrow his car to go get something to eat. Mr. Majestyk said he could eat with him, cold cuts and potato salad. Ryan said thanks, but he had to get some things at the drugstore anyway, so he might as well grab a bite in town.

He didn't stop in Geneva Beach. He headed directly for the migrant camp and pulled up next to the shed. Billy Ruiz, his face opening up when he saw Ryan, was alone inside.

Ryan looked around the room. He said, "Why didn't you put the beer case where I told you, behind the store?"

The surprised expression remained on Billy Ruiz's face and Ryan said, "Where is it?"

"Frank said he got rid of it that night. He said it would be better at night."

"Where is he?"

"I tole you, he was fired."

"I heard he was going to drive Camacho's bus back for him."

Billy Ruiz frowned. "Why? He got his truck."

"I heard his truck was busted."

"It's always busted, but he make it run. You think he leave it here?"

"Who's driving the bus, then?"

"I don't know. We got a new crew leader, he pick somebody knows how to drive it."

"Then, you're all set," Ryan said.

"Sure we get paid tomorrow, go home. Come up next year, hey, maybe we see you!"

"Maybe," Ryan said. "You never know."

On the way back he decided why not grab a bite. He stopped at Estelle's, then went over to the Pier Bar and had a couple while he watched the sun go down. It was a good place.

FIFTEEN

A FEW MINUTES BEFORE NINE NANCY UN-dressed and put on a pair of shorty pajamas. She left a lamp on in the bedroom, then went downstairs and turned off every light on the living room level, including the kitchen; she made sure the back door was double-locked. The door of the activities room, downstairs, was also locked. The only unlocked door in the house was the sliding door from the sun deck into the living room. She slid it silently open and closed it again.

Now the big chair with the ottoman. She pushed it over a little so it would be more in line with the door, closer but still in shadow, then worked the ottoman over. It was big and square and heavy, without casters; she could sit down in the chair and prop her feet against the inside edge of the ottoman and it was heavy enough that it wouldn't move away.

She sat down now and put her hand on the table next to the chair. She took her hand away and put it on the table again and moved the lamp over a few inches.

He could come anytime now. She had told him 9:30. He could be late if he had gone to The Pier and had to walk back or had trouble getting a ride. On the other hand there was a good chance he would be early. Eagerly early. There was no question in Nancy's mind that he would come. He had been coming back since Tuesday night and after last night she considered Jack Ryan nailed down. He could pose and declare his independence, but

180

he was like all the rest of them basically and she couldn't imagine him passing up a sure thing.

She began thinking about tomorrow and tried to imagine the look on Ray's face when he heard what happened. She could picture his expression when he walked in, the grim look. It would be hard not to laugh, or at least smile.

Right now, though, she'd better look alive and be ready and keep her eyes on the yard beyond the dark shape of the swimming pool. The only outside light was the orange bug lamp. He would pass through it as he approached the house.

"Hey, where you going?" Mr. Majestyk was standing at the edge of his front lawn. Behind him, past the thin birch trees, the spotlight held the flamingoes and painted stones in silent glare.

"I thought it was you," Mr. Majestyk said.

Ryan walked over. "I was just going up the beach."

Mr. Majestyk was lighting a cigar, puffing on it and shaking out the kitchen match. "The ball game's on. I was watching it over to Fisher's, but they're putting the kids to bed."

"Who'd you say, Baltimore?"

"Boston."

"That's right, McLain's going. Maybe I'll stop in later."

"No score in the second," Mr. Majestyk said. He added, almost without a pause, "Your buddy was here about an hour ago."

"Who's that?"

"Bob Junior." Mr. Majestyk drew on the cigar, watching Ryan. "He says he saw you up at the hunting property and thought you were trespassing."

"Is that what he said?"

"He says you told him you worked here and he was checking on it."

"You tell him I did?"

"You work here, don't you? I told him you and him should have a couple of beers sometime and cut out the crap."

181

"I can see that happening."

"He isn't a bad guy." Ryan was silent and Mr. Majestyk said, "What about the property? What do you think of it?"

"I don't know. It looks okay."

"You see the possibilities?"

"Well, he said he got himself a buck right there with an O-three, so maybe it's a good spot."

Mr. Majestyk squinted in his cigar smoke. "What were you doing, for Christ sake, fighting or having a conversation?"

"I guess it was a funny situation," Ryan said.

"It sounds it. Listen, I want to see the ball game, you stop in if you want." He puffed on the cigar a couple of times, watching Ryan walk off into the darkness. Finally, taking his time, he crossed the lawn to his house.

Ryan walked past the vacant frontage a good fifty yards before he had thought about it long enough and stopped. He looked out at the lake, at the distant pinpoints of light. He looked back toward Mr. Majestyk's house, at the garden and the flamingoes in the glow of the spot. He could see the side window, a square of light, where he and Nancy had looked in. Not a Western tonight, the ball game, the guy sitting there with a beer and not taking his eyes off the set. Ryan waited a couple more minutes before making up his mind.

He cut across the vacant frontage then and approached the side of the house, hearing the TV and recognizing the announcer's voice—George Kell, with the faintly downhome Arkansas drawl—before he reached the window and saw the picture and Mr. Majestyk watching it, his short legs stretched out on the fold-out ottoman.

Boston was at bat. McLain was pitching, looking in and taking his windup and coming in with a hard overhand fastball, grooving it past the hitter before he could swing. George Kell, sounding pretty relaxed, said it was McLain's fourth strikeout in three innings. He said boy, when this youngster was on, you just didn't hit him. Ryan watched the Tigers go out one two three in the fourth. With Boston coming to bat and McLain taking his

182

warm-up throws, he decided, what the hell, sit down for maybe a couple of innings. There wasn't any rush.

Since five o'clock Frank Pizarro had finished two bottles of red and almost half a fifth of vodka—vodka because the goddamn store didn't have any more tequila, the guy saying, "The way you people have been buying it . . ." Screw the guy, they would leave in a couple of days and the guy would wonder where his business went.

He had meant to save the vodka, to bring a whole bottle, but the goddamn wine made him feel tired an hour later and he used the vodka to get some life back in him. He felt good now and saw everything sharply, the houses in the darkness, the lights in the windows through the trees. He felt good, but he wished he had a cigarette.

The girl would have a cigarette. Plenty. Maybe Ryan would be there and he would have to wait. It didn't matter. Ryan would leave sometime and Mr. Ritchie's and Mr. Ryan's girl friend would be alone. How about Mr. Ritchie's and Mr. Ryan's and Mr. Pizarro's girl friend? He could show her something she had never seen before with any Mr. Ritchie or Jack goddamn Ryan.

He would wait and when it was only the girl—what could she do about it? But it would be better if he didn't have to wait.

He would come out of the shadow of the house and bushes and see the girl in the swimming pool, her dark hair and her body shining in the water. He would take the vodka and sit at the table this time and raise the bottle when she came out of the water.

No, save the vodka. Have her towel. She would come over with her hands on her hips and see him holding the towel. He would get up then and say to her, "Here, let me dry you," holding the goddamn towel open like a bull-fighter.

Jesus, Pizarro thought. He could feel her coming into his arms as he put the towel around her.

Get her nice and comfortable in there. He would be fooling around a little drying her and she would be laughing, putting her head back against his shoulder, and he would mention it to her then. "I want you to give me five

183

hundred dollars." And she would say, "Why should I give you five hundred dollars?" And you say, "Because if you don't, I tell somebody what you been doing with Jack Ryan." She say, "What somebody?" and you say, "Mr. Ray Ritchie somebody."

But the goddamn house looked dark, like nobody was home. He had parked on the other side of the Shore Road and walked into the Pointe. It was the house, he was sure of that; but no light showed anywhere on this side. Then go around, he told himself.

But what if Ryan was sitting by the pool and heard him? He had been lucky the time before; Ryan wasn't there. But if he came up from the beach side of the house —sure, he would be able to look the place over better. He could go to the next street and follow it to the beach and come around that way. If she wasn't home, that might be all right too. He could wait or he could go in and look around. Sure, maybe Mr. Ritchie kept some tequila somewhere.

"You ready?" Mr. Majestyk asked.

Ryan was sitting forward on the couch. He picked up the beer can between his feet and jiggled it. "Not yet."

"You know where it is." Mr. Majestyk sat back in his chair to watch the game and for a moment was silent.

"What's the count?"

"One and one."

"Two away, a man on second, the tieing run at the plate," Mr. Majestyk said. "How would you pitch this guy?"

"Probably something breaking. Low and away from him." Ryan watched the Boston hitter foul off the next pitch, a tapper down to the third base coaching box.

"He's not going to hit it," Mr. Majestyk said.

Ryan kept his eyes on the set. "I don't know. That short left field wall, you lay a fly ball up there, you got two bases."

And George Kell, a voice coming out of the TV set, said, "You got to pitch to everybody in this ballpark."

"In tight on the hands," Mr. Majestyk said. "Back the son of a bitch away. If he swings, he hits it on the handle."

"He better keep it low," Ryan said.

When the batter bounced out to the second baseman, Mr. Majestyk said, "I told you."

George Kell said, "Going into the sixth with a two-run lead, let's see if the Tigers can put some hits together and get something going. I imagine Denny McLain wouldn't mind that about now."

"He's good," Mr. Majestyk said. "You know?"

"Kell," Ryan said. "He was a good ballplayer."

"You know, he got over two thousand base hits while he was in the Majors?"

"Two thousand fifty-two," Ryan said.

"Did you know they had a sign outside his hometown? Swifton, Arkansas. You're coming in the sign says 'Swifton, Arkansas—The Home of George Kell.'"

Ryan took a sip of beer. "I don't know if I'd want a sign like that. Some guy comes along, he knows you're away playing ball, nobody home, he goes in takes anything he wants. Or you're in a slump and some nut fan throws rocks at your windows."

"That could happen," Mr. Majestyk said. "But when a guy is good, like Kell, you got to be able to take a lot of crap and not let it bother you. So a guy throws a rock. So you get the window fixed. Listen, you hit three thirty, three forty like Kell, the pitchers are throwing crap and junk at you all the time and it's worse than any rocks because it's your living, it's what you *do*. You stand in there, that's all. When they come in with a good one, you belt it."

"Or wait them out," Ryan said.

"Sure, or wait them out. But either way you got to stand in there. Maybe if you'd stayed in," Mr. Majestyk said then, "I mean, in baseball, maybe they'd be putting a sign up for you one of these days."

"Sure."

"I mean if you didn't have the bad back."

"You want to know something?" Ryan said, "Even if I didn't have it, I never could hit a goddamn curve ball."

Nancy saw the movement at the far end of the lawn: the figure briefly in the orange light and out of it, out of sight for a moment, now moving across the yard to the

deep shadows of the pines, and her finger continued
stroke the edge of her hair, down across her brow. S
sat comfortably with her feet on the inside edge of the c
toman, her knees up in front of her. She didn't move. S
wondered momentarily why he was being so sneaky abo
it. All he had to do was walk across the yard to tł
house. When she saw him again near the swimming poc
her right hand came away from her face.

The hand dropped to the side table and, without grop
ing, curved around the hard, smooth handle of her targe
pistol.

Nancy waited. She began to wonder if he had circled t
the back of the house. There was no reason he woulc
unless he wanted to look at the garage or the street, ju:
to be sure. There were no sounds, inside or out.

She waited, because she knew he would appear agair
She also knew—sitting, facing the sliding glass door tha
was sixteen feet from the front edge of her chair, her eye
on the glass now and not moving from it—exactly wha
she was going to do.

There were no sounds. Then a faint sound. A scrapin;
sound on the wooden stairs. She saw his head appear, a
dark shape against the sundeck, his shoulders, his body
He stood for a moment looking down at the yard. As hε
turned to the door Nancy brought the pistol up in front o'
her and laid the barrel on her raised knees. As he openec
the door, sliding the glass gently, and started to come inside, Nancy said, "Hi, Jackie."

She heard him say, "Is—" or something that soundeċ
like that but no more. With the pistol held straight in
front of her at eye level, held on him dead center, she
fired four times and continued to fire as he stumbled back
to the sun deck and went down, and she would have
sworn she heard the sound of glass breaking on the patio,
as if someone had dropped a glass or a bottle.

Nancy pulled herself out of the chair she had been sitting in for over an hour. She walked out to the sun deck
wondering if his eyes would be open or closed.

"What're they taking McLain out for? Jesus Christ, a
couple of hits and they pull him."

"They were hard-hit balls," Ryan said. "Both of them."

"So they get a hold of a couple."

"The leading run on second," Ryan said, "they got to be careful. Say, you know what time it is?"

Mr. Majestyk looked at his watch. "Quarter of ten. I'd leave him in. How many hits they got off him?"

"About six."

"Six hits. What—all singles? You don't hit this guy solid."

They watched the manager walk back to the dugout. McLain remained on the mound, throwing the ball into the pocket of his glove.

George Kell said, "Well, it looks like Denny's staying in. He's got his work cut out for him now. Two on, the potential leading run on second."

Mr. Majestyk was pulling himself out of his reclining chair. "The best part," he said, "and I got to take a leak. You need a beer while I'm up?"

"I'm all set."

"You want a highball? Whatever you want."

"I was supposed to meet somebody at nine thirty," Ryan said.

Mr. Majestyk swung his feet down. "I thought you already met her."

"No, I was going to. Then I thought I'd see a couple of innings first."

"Is she going to be sore at you?"

"I don't know."

"Do you care?"

"Well, I ought to talk to her sometime."

"It's up to you."

"I better do it," Ryan said. "Get it over with."

Someone, Nancy decided, should do a piece on Jack Ryan for the *Reader's Digest*. "The Luckiest Character I Have Ever Met in My Whole and Entire Life."

At first, looking down at Frank Pizarro, she was startled, disappointed, and finally angry. But, she decided, as she dragged Frank into the living room and slid the door closed, it wasn't all bad. This one deserved it as much as Ryan. She had to be philosophical, accept minor disap-

pointments like a big girl. She didn't have Ryan, but s
had his buddy, and the buddy should serve the purpo
just as well. He was dead and she had killed him.

The trouble was, she wasn't sure if windows were
more fun after all.

She turned on every light in the living room, then t
kitchen light and the desk lamp in the den. She picked
the telephone, then put it down and moved quickly to t
table next to the big chair. She had almost forgotten t
props. She took her wallet, a watch, a pearl necklace, an
several pins from the table drawer and stuffed them in
Frank's pockets. In her mind she heard a policeman o
someone say, "He was in your room?" And her ow
voice answering, "I heard him, but I didn't make a soun
I waited. I didn't go downstairs until I thought he'd gon
I don't know what made me take the gun. I'd bought
and I was going to give it to my boss as a present. M
Ritchie." She smiled at this touch. Great. Especially if
got in the papers word for word. "My boss." Or "Uncl
Ray." That might be better.

Nancy was in the den, once more about to dial th
phone, standing just inside the door and looking out int
the living room and this time when she replaced th
phone, she stepped back inside, out of the doorway.

Wow. Jackie was coming in from the sun deck.

She gave him time to take a good look at Frank Pizarro. She took a breath and let it out slowly and
straightened the V-neck of her shorty pajamas and
stepped into the living room as Ryan was getting up from
his knees. She watched him step over Frank Pizarro's legs
and saw his gaze raise abruptly.

"Late again," Nancy said. "Aren't you?"

"I guess I am," Ryan said. "Do you know he's dead?"

She nodded and was aware of Ryan's gaze holding on
her. "He came to ask for more money," Nancy said. "If I
didn't give it to him, he said he'd tell the police about
you."

"You had a conversation and then you shot him."

"When he came at me. After."

"You happened to have a gun."

188

"When he knocked," Nancy said. "I didn't know who was, so I got the gun first."

"Have you called the police?"

"Not yet."

"What're you going to tell them?"

She kept her gaze locked with his. "That I shot a rowler."

"Then, tomorrow," Ryan said, "your picture's in the aper."

"I didn't think of that."

"You might even get it in a magazine. *Life* maybe."

"Do you think so?"

"You wear dark glasses wherever you go and people oint to you and say, 'That's the one.'"

"Really?"

"Somebody in Hollywood sees the nice-looking little girl with the nice little can and the long hair who shot a nan in her millionaire boyfriend's beach house and you're there."

"Hey, neat."

"Ray's in a mess because his wife and everybody knows what he's been doing, but you can't worry about Ray now, can you?"

"Those are the breaks," Nancy said.

"You wouldn't need any fifty thousand. You shoot a cucumber picker and find happiness."

"Sort of a Cinderella story," Nancy said. "I like it." She seemed to be picturing it, nodding, as she stepped in front of the big chair and eased into it, sliding low in the seat.

"How many times did you shoot him?"

"I don't know. I didn't count."

"You shot him coming in."

"No, I heard him. But I didn't come out of my room until I thought he had gone. Then when I got downstairs, he was waiting for me."

"You shot Frank coming in the door," Ryan said. "Seven times. He didn't knock. He walked in."

Nancy put on a little surprised look. "That's right. Because I left the door open for you. But he did knock."

"What I mean," Ryan said, "you didn't mean to k
Frank."

"Of course I didn't mean to *kill* him."

"You thought it was me coming in."

"Sure."

"You meant to kill me."

Nancy sat quietly in the chair. "I did huh—why?"

"I guess there are a lot of reasons," Ryan said. "B
mainly because you thought it would be fun." He waite
moving to the ottoman and sitting down in front of her.

"Was it?"

"It was all right."

"But not what you thought it would be."

"Isn't that funny?"

Her eyes followed him as he rose now and moved to
ward the den. "Where are you going?"

"Call the police."

"I'll do it."

"You might get it wrong."

"You tell on me, Jackie, I'll tell on you."

Ryan paused in the doorway. He felt tired and shook
his head slowly. He said, "Hey, come on, okay?"

"I mean it. I'll say you were with him. I'll tell them
about the wallets."

"All right," Ryan said. "You tell them about the wallets."

He went into the den and picked up the phone and she
heard him say to the operator, "I'm calling the state police." There was a long silence. She heard him say, "I
want to report a shooting," and a silence again. Then the
sound of words: "Out at the Pointe . . . Ray Ritchie's
place. . . . Huh? . . . No, you'll see when you get here."

As he came out to the living room she said, "All right
for you, Jackie. Boy are you going to get it."

With his foot Ryan pushed the ottoman over to the
walnut console model TV that he could get a hundred
and a half for and fooled with the dials until the picture
came clearly into focus to show McLain still in there.
George Kell said, "Two on, two out, top of the ninth."
Ryan eased down on the ottoman.

Nancy leaned over the arm of the big chair to watch him for long seconds, almost a minute.

"Jackie?" she said, and waited. "Jack, you nifty lover, hey. What if I tell them you came in and surprised him and you had a fight. Do you see it? You even *look* like you were in a fight."

Nancy waited.

"I'll tell them you saved my life. You pulled him off me and—listen—while you were fighting I got the gun. Then he was about to hit you with something, the poker, and I had to shoot him."

Her eyes opened with the little surprised look. "Hey, Jack, then we *both* get our pictures in the paper. And in *Life*—a big picture of us wearing real neat sunglasses. And then both of us get in the movies! Wouldn't that be it?" She opened her mouth and her eyes, faking it a little but actually taken with the idea.

Ryan looked at her. He waited until he was sure she was watching him and listening and he said, "I've been in the movies."

He looked back at the TV set, at McLain bringing up his leg and throwing from the shoulder with a man on base. The son of a bitch was good, but he could sure get in trouble.

"Listen, I'm serious," Nancy said. "It can work. It would be more fun with somebody else." She waited, watching him. "Listen to me, will you? Look at me. This could be great. We tell them what happened and in a couple of days we take the car and go—wherever you want, just go. Jack, listen to me!"

McLain looked over at the runner on first, paused, and delivered his pitch. "Fastball inside and a little high," George Kell said.

"We can make it look good," Nancy said. She paused, thoughtful, before pushing herself out of the chair. "We'll say he was violent. In fact"—her hands went to the V-neck of her shorty pajamas—"before I got to the gun, he grabbed me and tore my pajamas off." Her hands came down, ripping the front of the pajama top to the hem. She held it open and said, "Jackie, look what he did."

Ryan looked. He nodded and looked back at the set again.

Nancy was thoughtful for a moment. "Then, all of sudden, he went psycho and started smashing things."

She used the poker from the fireplace, bringing it u swinging at the painting over the mantel, hacking at and smashing the light fixture. She destroyed a glass cabi net in the living room and worked her way into the dinin room, smashing every piece of glass and crystal and chin she saw: vases, ashtrays, figurines, a mirror vanished in a sound of splintered glass. She shattered the entire floor to-ceiling thermopane that faced the sun deck, choppin away the fragments of glass that pointed jaggedly out o the frame. She saved the lamps until last, smashing then one by one, the room becoming dim and finally dark Only the flat white glow of the TV picture remained.

A silence followed. Nancy stood near the big chair ir her torn shorty pajamas. She stood motionless, the silence lengthened, and the voice of George Kell said, "All tied up in the bottom of the ninth with Detroit coming to bat. If they're going to put something together now's the ——"

Ryan turned off the sound. He sat hunched in the white glow of the picture tube. Behind him, Al Kaline silently swung two bats in the on-deck circle.

He said to her, "Have you broken everything?"

She seemed to nod. "I guess so."

"Then, why don't you sit down?"

"Jackie——"

"No more, all right? If you say any more, I think I'll bust you one and I don't want to do that."

As Al Kaline stepped into the batter's box and took his stance, touching the end of the bat to the plate and digging a foothold with his spikes, they heard the first thin sound of the siren far up the Shore Road.

"Sit down and relax," Ryan said. "There's nothing more to think about."

Nancy curled slowly into the chair, leaning on one of the arms and resting her face in her hand. She stared out at the swimming pool and the lawn and the orange pinpoint of light against the night sky and a finger began stroking the soft, falling edge of her dark hair.